MW01247040

Thia Lynne has a degree in elementary education from Indiana University and a master of special education from Grand Canyon University. Since retiring from teaching students with various disabilities, she is pursuing writing books that involve people who face seemingly insurmountable difficulties including emotional problems, death of loved ones, disabled children and Alzheimer's disease. Most of the subject matter is drawn from her own life experiences and from those with whom she has dealt. She lives in a small, out of the way town in Texas with her wonderful husband, Bruce, and their amazing dog, Boaz. There are several cats running about too. She has grown children and grandchildren in wide flung locations.

This is a work of fiction. Names, characters, businesses, places, events and incidents are either the product of the author's imagination or used in a fictitious manner. Any resemblance to actual persons, living or dead, or actual events is purely coincidental.

Escape From Rest Haven

Thia Lynne

Escape From Rest Haven

Vanguard Press

VANGUARD PAPERBACK

© Copyright 2024
Thia Lynne

The right of Thia Lynne to be identified as author of
this work has been asserted by her in accordance with the
Copyright, Designs and Patents Act 1988.

All Rights Reserved

No reproduction, copy or transmission of this publication
may be made without written permission.
No paragraph of this publication may be reproduced,
copied or transmitted save with the written permission of the
publisher, or in accordance with the provisions
of the Copyright Act 1956 (as amended).

Any person who commits any unauthorised act in relation to
this publication may be liable to criminal
prosecution and civil claims for damages.

A CIP catalogue record for this title is
available from the British Library.

ISBN 978-1-83794-051-6

Vanguard Press is an imprint of
Pegasus Elliot Mackenzie Publishers Ltd.
www.pegasuspublishers.com

First Published in 2024

Vanguard Press
Sheraton House Castle Park
Cambridge England

Printed & Bound in Great Britain

I dedicate this book to my mother, Rebecca Terrell, who gave the inspiration for the Alzheimer's sufferer in this story. She is no longer constrained by her failing body.

Thank you to my sister Kathy Chambers for reading this book, giving encouragement, and correcting my poor memory. April Morgan did an early reading of my manuscript and had many helpful suggestions, so thank you, my dear old friend. A final read-through caught even more of my errors, so thank you to my dear new friend, Sarah Dodson. I especially want to thank my biggest fan, my husband, Bruce Allen, who never has a discouraging word. What would I do without you?

Chapter One

Anna walked into the old trailer home and looked around. The place was falling apart. There was nothing here of value. Mama was a hoarder — and a messy one at that. Filthy. The place smelled of dogs, cats, various woodland creatures and all of their excrement. How would she ever clean this up? To start, she would need a mask and gloves. Her eyes started watering. She couldn't tell if it was the smell or something else.

Stepping around and through the piles of boxes, while trying to avoid holes in the floor that had been creatively covered with old highway signs, was an adventure she wasn't enjoying. The yield sign appeared much larger on the hall floor than it would in its correct location on the roadside. As she entered Mama's bedroom, another sign looked like it said 'Welcome to Louisiana', but she couldn't be sure because of the piles of clothes and old books lying on it.

Anna began her laborious tour of the trailer. She was the one who constantly had to come to the rescue. She was the oldest, and that's what the oldest child did. The youngest was Alice, who had developed the enviable ability to stay out of family business. Her name, and those of her siblings, all began with A, probably Mama's way of bringing about some sort of family unity. Andrew was in the middle and made travel to far-away places his priority from the time he finished high school. Sometimes he could be reached and sometimes he couldn't, depending maybe on circumstances, but probably more on his own wise inclinations.

Anna opened a box and peered inside at the faded magazines and scraps of torn-out pages from periodicals. They were all the publications commonly known as women's magazines. She remembered how Mama always seemed to be reading them. She sometimes enjoyed the magazines herself until Mama snatched random publications away from her. Her mother probably had some interest in fashion and cosmetics — but recipes?

Mama was not much of a cook, leaving most of that to Daddy. She did try her hand at it when absolutely necessary, but the results never reflected much care and attention, so the abundance of torn-out recipes jumbled up in containers was certainly puzzling. Scraps of mysterious ads depicted no order or reason. Recipes and old family photographs were haphazardly piled in the boxes. Some of them were certainly of sentimental value, so why were they all jumbled up with such trash? Anna could only shrug her shoulders and think, *That's Mama.*

"Argh!" She let out a piercing scream as an enormous rodent raced across the toe of her shoe and into the bathroom. It was only a possum, but that knowledge didn't arrest her shaking knees. Thank goodness it wasn't a rat.

Anna hated rats, but she knew that possums ate unwanted insects and didn't carry rabies. This one scurried down through an air-conditioning vent in the bathroom floor. The vent cover was off, and its current location was just another unreasonable mystery. The trailer was a better home for a possum than for a human.

Anna decided that there was very little of value that could be salvaged from the entire mess. From the ceiling ruined by water damage to the floor ruined by pets and hard living, she wondered how she would ever sort through the chaos. Maybe she shouldn't even try but just call in someone else to scrap the whole thing and keep whatever they could out of the raw materials as payment. She certainly didn't want it. Some memories were best forgotten. Maybe a match and some sort of accelerant would be the right solution. *No!* What was she thinking? It was against the law to deliberately start a house fire even in a derelict trailer. She had never been one to color outside the lines, so she wasn't going to start now.

As she did a final perusal before she headed for the exit, she caught a glimpse of an unusual item in the corner of the extra bedroom. *No way! A computer? What on earth would Mama be doing with a computer?* Her skill set had certainly never included technology. Anna had to push back a loaded clothes rack, a pile of old shoes, a huge collection of classic CD movies that went crashing to the floor in every direction, and a stack of boxes seemingly filled with old magazine clippings, in order to reach the table holding the computer. More magazines and stacks of file folders were heaped on the table, across the keyboard, and on top of the computer.

Anna began opening the manila folders. She was stunned into a stupor when she saw the shocking, unexplainable images they contained. Her heart began to pound, and her hands shook so violently that she could barely focus on the horrors detailed in the pages. Anna dropped the folder and screamed louder than when she'd encountered the possum.

After she had collected herself to a degree, though her heart was still racing and her knees hadn't stopped shaking since the rodent incident, she rummaged through folder after folder and found that they were all similar except for the individuals depicted. Anna shoved a stack of magazines off the chair in front of the table and cleared the other papers off the keyboard. Starting the computer up terrified her, but she felt driven by incredulity and an intense need to know.

When the box popped up for the password, Anna frowned. Her daddy had always chided her for frowning so much, and Mama assured her that she would be prematurely wrinkled. It was funny how that thought came to her at this crucial time. She wondered what would be an appropriate password for Mama. What was most important to her? She was suddenly struck by the sad fact that she didn't know what mattered to her own mother, especially since now she seemed an absolute stranger. On a whim, Anna typed in 'AAA123!!!'. Mama had frequently

referred to her children as the three-As. The computer immediately opened.

The strangeness of such a silly password caused her to laugh until her stomach hurt and her eyes streamed with tears. It was a relief to laugh away some of her hysteria. Who would look at that password and think anything but about the company that protected people from vehicular breakdowns and gave travel help? But Anna knew that it was the first initial in the names of Mama's three children. So, in spite of everything, they had mattered to her after all, at least enough to use them for a password. Or maybe they were more — perhaps just part of a cover?

Chapter Two

Anna thought back to the draining experience of getting Mama into the nursing home. Mama had shrieked at the orderly who was trying to remove her from the car. He tried reasoning with her but got nowhere. He finally scooped her up, at which she kicked and flailed so much he lost his footing and was just able to plop her into the wheelchair before he hit the asphalt and rolled like a stunt man.

Anna had lied to her endlessly in the preceding few weeks because she was so uncooperative and refused to acknowledge that she had Alzheimer's, even when she was lost wandering down her street before dawn. Still, the process required to get her finally admitted had taken several months.

Anna felt like her nerves were shot with the whole ordeal. She had gone to her doctor to ask for a prescription for anxiety just so she could shut her mind off at night in order to get some rest. She had always considered herself a strong person, but persistently lying to Mama had taken its toll on her nerves.

In desperation, she tried for days until she reached her sister, Alice. "I haven't lied to Mama this much since we were teenagers!" They had laughed together. This simple

18

contact with her estranged sister seemed to lighten the load just a little. Then they lost contact again, and Anna felt desolate.

"You don't know what you're doing!" Mama had continued to scream. "They'll come after me. They'll come after all of us. You don't break the rules of The Cooking School!"

More irrationality. Anna had never had contact with anyone with Alzheimer's disease before, and the effects had blindsided her. Mama had berated her, called her names, accused her of stealing, and steadily tried to ruin her reputation with everyone they knew. She no longer felt she could call on family or friends because of how they must certainly feel about her from the things Mama had told them, except Alice. Mama didn't know how to get in touch with Alice. She was the only safe one.

When Mama was first diagnosed, everyone asked how the doctor could tell because she had always acted like there was something a bit off with her mental health anyway. Daddy, a light airplane pilot and crop-duster, had always been the stability in the family.

As soon as he walked in the door after work, he rounded up his three children and began the regular activity of supervising the house cleaning, cooking and gardening. During this process, Mama could usually be found with a magazine or staring off into space with a cigarette and a cup of coffee. Occasionally, the coffee was replaced by a glass of Mogen David.

Secrets could be strange things. They tended to pile up like the detritus accumulated in Mama's trailer. She was always secretive. Anna only started suspecting the reasons slowly as she matured. Year by year, understanding dawned, and with that understanding grew her sense of disdain. First, she no longer allowed her mother's hugs. These had begun to somehow feel dirty. Then, she learned to be an expert liar. One lie deserved another, didn't it?

The episodes generally started with the arrival of Aunt Edith. She would show up unexpectedly, stay a couple of days, and then she and Mama would disappear just as unexpectedly. They typically stayed gone from a few days to occasionally a month.

Aunt Edith was lots of fun. She always arrived with her son Pierce, both of them squeezing through the door laden down with gifts for all the children. Pierce fit in like he belonged with the family, and Daddy accepted his presence as such. Apparently, Pierce was accustomed to being placed in various situations since his mom was constantly traveling. As a result, he was home-schooled and arrived with his learning materials packed into suitcases that also contained activities and snacks — always prepared.

Edith played games with the children during the day and holed up with Mama in her basement study long into the night. Daddy was the one taking care of all the practical needs like preparing food and making sure everyone brushed their teeth and did their schoolwork. This seemed perfectly normal to a young child.

Chapter Three

Thankfully the computer used Windows, a system Anna was familiar with. She looked at all the yellow folder icons and noticed that they had titles showing cuisine from various countries around the world, Indian, Spanish, Russian, Lebanese, and then there was American and British. Anna opened the Russian folder first and found that it was all written in Russian with various files within the files. She closed it and opened the Spanish. It was set up just like the Russian one with all the files labeled in Spanish. She then opened the British one and read the list of folders titled by people's names. She opened another and saw that they were exactly like the hard copy folders she had seen stacked on the table.

She pressed the print icon and heard a printer trying to operate under a stack of small boxes that had apparently once contained various cleaning items — a spin mop, a Swiffer duster set, and some other 'sold only on TV' specialty items guaranteeing a clean house.

Ha! That's a laugh! She knocked the boxes off the printer that was now spitting out the terrifying photos. Looking around in hopes of finding a shredder, she barely heard the ring tone from the cell phone in her purse. Where was that purse now? It seemed an eternity since she had sat it down next to the front door.

She didn't try to run since she knew voicemail would pick up before she could get it. The tone started again so she dropped the offensive pictures and stomped toward the intrusive noise. She picked it up just as it stopped ringing. The call log indicated that it was the nursing home where Mama was in care. The voicemail tone dinged so she put it on speaker and connected to voicemail. The harried voice of the nursing home director told her that she must call them at once. Anna's reaction was to huff out a breath and say, "What now?"

Anna heard the sound of the phone ringing and ringing at Rest Haven Nursing Home. Rest Haven! It sounded more like a cemetery name than one for a nursing home. She knew it was the phone at the nursing station, which was arbitrarily answered should someone deign to pick it up. When the bored CNA answered, Anna said she had gotten a call concerning Mama and was told to call back immediately. "Hold on!" was all Anna heard and then the phone went dead. The longer she waited the more impatient she felt. Mama had put her through the wringer ever since Aunt Edith informed her that Mama needed to see a neurologist.

Mama had been scammed. She was contacted by someone from South Africa telling her she had won $250,000. All she had to do was send them $900 so they could handle her international processing and it would be over-nighted to her. She was given step by step instructions to go to the bank, write a check for cash, take the cash to the store, purchase a group of $100 prepaid Visa cards, and FedEx them to the address the caller provided. This started a chain reaction of bounced checks. Because she was on a limited income, she couldn't even buy groceries. She seemed to have no shame in asking Aunt Edith for money. After a couple of months, with continued outlandish expenditures and unable to catch her up financially, Edith called Anna and gave her the news.

When the neurologist informed Anna that Mama had Alzheimer's disease, Anna was able to have the bank refund her overdraft charges and put Mama back on her feet with just a little extra help from Anna's savings, money she sacrificed from her small business. Anna then went to Social Security and took care of the paperwork to become Mama's designated payee, so she could make sure that Mama's bills were paid and that she had enough left over for groceries and spending money.

In her irrational state, Mama decided that Anna was stealing from her and proceeded to tell anyone who would listen that her daughter was a thief who was cheating her out of all of her wealth. When Anna tried to explain the situation, Mama told her that she did not, under any definition of the term, have Alzheimer's and that Anna had made the doctor say she did so she could take over her funds. No amount of reasoning and proof would shake her assertion.

Anna had turned her own life upside down to liquidate her business and move from Indiana to Louisiana to look after her mother. She thought of the torment her mother had put her though and the ridiculousness of the accusation as she stood looking at the pitiful mess that was Mama's home. All this played through her head while she was waiting for someone to come to the phone and explain what the call was about.

The agitated nursing director finally came to the phone, sounding out of breath. "I'm so, so sorry to tell you this, but we can't find your mother. No one saw her go and we've looked everywhere. We've contacted the local police and a search is underway."

Anna felt like she couldn't catch her breath. One minute she was rehashing her hurt and grievances against Mama and the next she was terrified that something might have happened to her.

Chapter Four

She was in the process of hurrying to her car to see what she could do to help in the search when a large, blue conversion van screeched into the driveway, spitting gravel. Anna stared at the unfamiliar vehicle in shock until her Aunt Edith jumped out of the driver's side door. How she managed to jump was quite a feat considering her age and how her formerly fit body had thickened over the years, but jump she did. Then she hustled toward Anna with her now pendulous breasts and mounding stomach jiggling before her in her surprisingly rapid progress. Anna felt glued to her spot on the rickety landing at the front door of the derelict trailer house. Then her eyes fixed on Edith's passenger. She didn't know if she should feel more anger or relief at seeing Mama sitting there gazing blankly out the windshield.

Mechanically, Anna started down the rotting steps toward Aunt Edith who began yelling and gesturing wildly, so Anna stopped in her tracks. As Edith mounted the stairs, she roughly pushed Anna back into the decrepit building. This was not the aunt she had known. What was happening?

Edith began spitting out orders as she started toward the bathroom with Anna following as if in a dream. When the authoritarian elderly woman got to the ventless bathroom floor air receptacle, she reached her arm inside. A loud grinding noise started, and the toilet tilted back into the wall, revealing stairs going down into a black hole. Edith looked at it and began pondering aloud. "No wonder she wasn't able to obtain protection. The years have been unkind."

"What are you talking about? What is this?" Anna was trembling all over. Everything was piling in on her and she was feeling like she was wading into dangerously deep water. Mama was still out in the van, which was worrisome in itself. Edith pushed her helpless companion through the hole in the floor, shouting at her to gather up all the supplies she could and send them up to her. Anna complied in numb confusion.

A light went on as she got to the bottom. She was in a room lined with cement and stacked high with shelves laden with an assortment of weapons Anna had never known existed. She was afraid to touch them, but with Edith's yelling and her concern that Mama was alone outside, she overcame her hesitancy and loaded a duffle bag that was conveniently hanging next to the shelf. She packed it with guns small enough to pick up and then hauled them up the steep stairs. When she got to the top, Edith quickly checked them out and then reprimanded her harshly for neglecting to collect ammunition.

Back down into the hole she went and scanned the overflowing shelves. "Where are they?" she yelled.

"Just look, girl! They are in little boxes with numbers on them."

Finally, Anna saw boxes marked '38' and '9MM'. "Are these OK?"

"Yes! Just load up all you can."

Frantically searching, she found another duffle bag in the corner and dumped in as many small cardboard boxes as she could fit. It was quite heavy, and it was all she could do to hoist it to the top and over the edge. As she climbed out, Edith was already heading for the door, adeptly maneuvering so as not to fall through the rotting floor.

Anna hurried behind her and scooped up her purse that had been dropped on the landing when she was pushed through the front door. She was thankful to see that Mama had stayed in the van. When she expressed this sentiment to Aunt Edith, all she heard was, "Child locks," as Edith continued in her determined activity.

"Help me, girl!" she yelled, carrying containers out of the back of the van and charging past into the house. As Anna approached, she smelled gasoline.

"We aren't!" she whined.

"Oh, yes we are!" came the response.

"Why? Why? Aunt Edith? What on earth is going on?"

"Open your eyes, girl. And please quit calling me Aunt Edith. I am neither your aunt nor Edith."

"What? This is just too much. I can't take it all in! Weapons, you, Mama, portfolios of dead people."

This stopped Edith, or whatever her name was, in her tracks. "What do you mean, portfolios of dead people?"

"All in the back room stacked in boxes and on top of every surface — dead people pictures, magazines, recipes, family photos, just piles and piles of crazy stuff!"

"This is worse than I thought," mumbled Edith, as she hauled what were obviously gasoline cans into the trailer. Anna caught up with her in the room with the pictures and heard her say, "Now I understand."

"Understand what?" asked Anna.

"Look. Your mom has dementia. She was losing things, passwords, procedures, everything. This was her attempt to hold onto what she might need. It's too late now, and all this stuff is just a liability. You're going to ram your car into the side of this trash heap and then we're going to run like… well, you know."

Aunt Edith knew never to curse around Anna. It was always Mama's rule no matter what happened. Somehow this little bit of sanity snapped Anna out of her state of confusion. It was evident that things were happening that were outside her field of understanding but were so critical in nature that she knew she should obey Aunt Edith, or whoever she was. Something was seriously wrong, but Aunt Edith was always strong and wise. She would know what to do. And then Anna heard her say, "I'll go out and get the body."

Chapter Five

Anna watched as Edith bounced her energetic self to the back of the van and pulled out a cart like the ones people use to haul groceries or laundry. She then started tugging on an unwieldy object that Anna couldn't quite identify, though there was something decidedly disturbing about the object. "Don't just stand there! There's work to do, and we're running out of time," Edith commanded.

Anna hurried over to lend a hand but then jumped back in horror. An emaciated elderly lady, carelessly wrapped in a sheet, was staring at her, arms and legs poking out at impossible angles.

"Yeah," Edith said. "Rigor's setting in, and it can do some crazy things to a body. Are you going to help me or just stand there?" Edith looked at Anna's sickly, pale face and realized she would have to handle this part of the operation herself.

It wasn't easy, but she managed to poke the body into the back seat of Anna's car. She couldn't get the door to shut but decided it probably wasn't necessary for their purposes. "Are you going to make me do everything? This is your mother I'm trying to save, after all. And in case you didn't know, this last part is to save your life too."

Anna shook her head and looked at Edith. "What?"

"You seem to be a little slow to grasp all this. I blame your mother for sheltering her little angel so much, sending you to services in that church van, watching our language... Anyway, you need to hop into this driver seat and ram your car into the house. Hopefully, that will ignite my little booby trap there and we can be off. It will take some time before anyone realizes the charred body in your car isn't you. The fire should obscure the body's location, especially if you hit the house hard enough and embed the car so everything gets mixed up real nice. The local yokels in this one cow town might never even figure it all out. You'll be declared dead, the unfruitful search for your missing mother will be covered up by the wealthy nursing home owner, and we can all breathe a little easier."

None of this made any sense, but the computer, the folders, the room with the weapons, made this last little bit at least fit some sort of crazy pattern. Anna stumbled awkwardly toward her car. She gunned the engine and hit the gas. The sooner she got this over with, the better. The impact crumpled the old trailer and it toppled on top of the car.

Edith was yelling, "Too fast! Oh no! That was too fast! Jump out of there and run!"

Anna barely heard her. She struggled to open her driver's door, but it was blocked by debris. Then she smelled smoke mixed with gasoline and realized that she might soon see the Jesus she had loved since childhood and who had always made her feel safe in the midst of the turmoil that was her life.

Anna looked around for a way to escape. She could still hear Edith yelling encouragement at her, but the words didn't make any sense in the midst of the encroaching fire and confusion. When she looked around for a way out, she saw the pathetic dead woman in the back seat with her feet sticking through the open car door. The only way out was to climb over the seat, over the body of the poor stranger, who would hopefully save her life, and make her way out of the toppled mess that was her mother's former home.

After untangling thick toenails from her hair, she flung herself from the car and onto the muddy ground that had been moldering under Mama's trailer for years. Then she crawled toward the gap of sunshine sending eerie waves through the smoke. When she reached the grass, she looked up and saw Edith with her arms crossed and an amused smile on her face. "I knew you could do it, girl. Your mama never gave you enough credit. She didn't challenge you like I did my Pierce. Now brush yourself off, and let's get out of here."

Chapter Six

Anna settled into one of the back bucket seats while Edith circled the van around to head south.

"Where are we going?" Anna inquired.

"Well," answered Edith, "speaking of Pierce." That's all Anna heard before her stomach started doing somersaults.

All those years growing up with Pierce coming and going from their lives produced memories that perpetually generated a pang in her heart. As childhood grew into adolescence, the friendship between them grew closer. They were thrown into the same situation and shared their secrets and suspicions about their mothers. When they entered adulthood, they recognized the fact that they were in love. They were horrified at the implications of cousins loving one another. They knew they could never have a future together. Stolen kisses in the dark hallway always felt like unforgivable sins. They were not immoral people, were they? No matter how it hurt, they knew their relationship had to end. They couldn't even be friends.

Anna was twenty and Pierce was twenty-two the last time they saw one another during a December college break.

The meeting was painful for so many reasons. The mix of longing, sadness and shame was more than they could deal with. They made a pact never to see one another again. After twenty years, and Anna's childless — well, nearly childless — disappointing marriage, she was going to see her cousin Pierce once more. How would her emotions be able to stand the strain in the midst of current circumstances?

Anna was roused from her musings by the sound of Mama's voice. She was asking Edith if she remembered their adventures as young, daring Marines. She was calling Edith Trident, and Edith was referring to Mama as Pelican. Were they pet names from their childhood? Very strange names if they were. Finally, Anna couldn't stand the silly talk any more and interrupted. "What's with the strange nicknames?"

Mama looked at Anna through the visor mirror and asked what she was talking about. "You know our code names, Captain. Is this another test? I'm getting tired of tests. Too old. Just stop, please." Then she closed her eyes and went to sleep. Anna shrugged off her mom calling her Captain. It was just more madness.

"You see why I had to get her out of there? What kind of insanity caused you, without even consulting me, to put your mother into a nursing home? Now, thanks to your stupidity, we are all in danger."

"I didn't know I needed to consult you!" Anna nearly shouted. "I haven't seen your face for twenty years. You abandoned me, us, my family! Except when you called to stop Mama from spending money. What kind of a sister are you? What gives you the right to demand staying in the loop of this tightrope I've had to walk alone dealing with my mother?"

"Well, girl, let's get a few things straight first. Did you not hear me when I said I'm not your aunt?"

"I heard you; I just don't believe you. I don't know what kind of game you're playing here, but I've known you my entire life and never, on any single day, did I believe that you're not my aunt and that Pierce isn't my cousin. And you still haven't explained the crazy nicknames."

"Anna. It's so funny hearing that name again. Did you know that you were named for me?"

"My name isn't Edith."

"Neither is mine. I've known your mother since we first met at Marine bootcamp. We were like sisters. We had very similar skillsets. Both of us were spot-on marksmen. or markswomen, whatever. Anyway, there were no women snipers in any branch of the service — officially. We were convoy drivers. We were right in the middle of the fray during Desert Storm. Everyone in our unit, outside of our chain of command, knew to ignore our activities when the convoy would stop, and we would take off to high ground to wait for the enemy. That group of supply trucks continued on their way. We did our job and hung around until the next convoy arrived at the subscribed point. We would then slip down the hillside and hop into a truck headed back to base.

"Your mom and I had lots of deep talks during that time. I wanted to take out Saddam Hussein, but Pelican thought he should stay put. As ruthless as he was, he was the only one who could keep all the warring clans somewhat on peaceful terms. He allowed religious liberty, too, something virtually unheard of in the Middle East. Turns out, in hindsight, your mom was right. Humph! That part of the world is such a mess, it seems like everything we do only ends up making it worse. We need to get out of everyone else's business and take care of our own here and now.

"But back in our younger days, we thought we knew best. We thought we had the moral high ground, so we could change the world for the better. But you know what, Anna? Turns out the world doesn't want to change into what we think would be better, things like peace and a future for our children. You like to think that everyone is sorta like you are, but the sad truth is, they aren't. How we can begin to understand what goes on in the minds of people who, from infancy, have never known anything but violence and war. It is the height of hubris. I've become a lot more of a 'live and let live' person in my old age. Acceptance of the inevitable is a whole lot easier to grow old with, and I do intend to grow old. Older, that is."

Anna found it hard to follow Edith's streaming narrative with Pierce on her mind. Pierce! He wasn't her cousin after all! What kind of life could they have had together had their parents only been honest with them? The sense of anger mixed with loss overwhelmed Anna. She dozed off from the latent stress as Edith continued talking about the good ol' days on the two-hour trip to New Orleans.

Chapter Seven

Things had been running fairly smoothly at The Cooking School for quite some time. Pierce was now one of the twelve leaders of the organization that had headquarters in various locations around the world. His base was at his restaurant, The Rice Bowl, located in New Orleans. It featured spicy, cleanly sourced cuisine with exotic rice varieties at its base — black rice, wild rice and even cauliflower rice for those who were on low-carb diets. He felt a little uncomfortable operating out of a location that drew civilians, but it was better than a school or a hospital where some of his associates were conducting operations.

He had an assortment of contingency plans, backup locations, for just such an emergency. He had been in the midst of preparing for the dinner crowd when he got the message that he had been expecting since the directive came out against his aunt.

Since he had entered college, he knew this aunt wasn't really his biological aunt, and that his cousin Anna wasn't really his cousin. He was directed to keep their secrets when his mother began opening up to him in his teens when it became evident that he had valuable skills. He was trained in Tai Kwando and archery from childhood. Then, he went on to become the head of his high school wrestling team and the state paint ball champion. He continued to broaden his horizons in kickboxing and some more obscure martial arts techniques.

He had been questioning his mother's disappearances from before he could remember. When he started to rebel, his mom went on a search and found some marijuana in his bedroom. With that, she realized it was time she leveled with him. What she said was like someone opening a curtain to mysteries long kept hidden. It turned his life upside down. But the answers caused everything to make sense. Pierce gained new respect for the single mother who had done her best to bring him up to be a strong, smart, independent man. It was with full approval of The Cooking School that this revelation was made. At that point, his formal training began.

It was hard for him to keep the secret about their real relationship the last time he saw Anna. She was already engaged to be married and was just earning her degree in architecture and interior design. He knew he wouldn't have a chance. Why upset her well-ordered world? It broke his heart.

Pierce shook his mind out of reveries of the past. His mom had contacted him to let him know that they were headed in his direction. He was going to see Anna again. And she was single! She was also in the middle of a crisis that would put even more strain on their long-fractured relationship. He strengthened his resolve to protect Anna from the most frightening aspects of the truth. He didn't know how that would be possible, but he would do all he could to continue to shield her. Now it was time to get busy with preparations, time to direct his thoughts to the task.

He downloaded and printed the pre-prepared door signs. The one for the restaurant said:

DUE TO A PRIVATE PARTY RENTING OUT
FACILITY, WE ARE CLOSED TO REGULAR
CUSTOMERS TONIGHT. PLEASE COME BACK
TOMORROW FOR A 10% DISCOUNT

He hoped circumstances would allow him to provide that discount. The more complicated part was next — calling customers with reservations and explaining that this was a mix-up on the part of the restaurant management and that they were very sorry. The reservation customers' names were documented, and they would be given a free meal at their next visit.

The next phase was preparing his backup location, the old church building on Camp Street. A small, aging congregation still met there on Sunday mornings. In years gone by, the large building had an active congregation with multiple Sunday school gatherings meeting in the basement. A basement is rare in New Orleans, but this building had one. The huge rooms had windows high in the walls that looked out at street level. Children used to play games during vacation Bible school, and the sounds of their laughter rang through the cavernous, cement expanse. That was many years ago.

Though the church was small, they had an efficient phone prayer chain. All it took was one call to start the process that was needed to ensure the safety of the fragile congregants. This call informed the members that the pastor was ill and that he coveted their prayers. Since they didn't have anyone to preach on Sunday, they were encouraged to pray and worship in their homes until further notice. Financial arrangements had already been made with the pastor. He had agreed to rely on his multiple physical maladies to take some time off to rest when he was called on to do so. All the expenses of running the church and allowing it to keep its doors open were taken care of by a benefactor. It was a no-lose agreement. The next phone call sealed the church's doors for the foreseeable future.

Chapter Eight

After napping about an hour, Mama woke up and began talking. Since she had started exhibiting signs of Alzheimer's disease, she kept repeating the same stories. One of her favorites was to go back through the details of giving birth to her three children. Her favorite story was the one about her son, Andrew. She recited that Andrew had been a big baby and that she was having a difficult labor. Anna had heard it all before, but since it seemed to make Mama happy to tell it again, Anna pretended like she was hearing it for the first time.

Daddy was trying to learn how to hypnotize people. Anna always laughed at the ridiculousness of this story. After a while, the doctor came in and saw what Daddy was doing and offered to take over. As Mama always told the story before, this doctor was an expert hypnotist, and his treatment eased her labor.

This time, she told the story differently. "The doctor was a trained operative and knew that I shouldn't be subjected to hypnosis by an amateur. He took over to protect our secrets. I was always attended by members of The Cooking School. They knew how to keep everything under wraps, even in the hospital, and even while I was giving birth."

Here again was this alternative life her mother was leading even that long ago.

Edith began to add to the story. "Since I was Pelican's handler, I was called on to back her up in these situations, but if I were to be delayed, there was always someone on hand to take care of whatever she needed."

Anna was beginning to see that this thing her mom had been involved in was way bigger than she could imagine. Nothing was as it appeared. "Edith," she began. "Can I call you Edith? It's all I've ever known you as."

"Make it easy on yourself," Edith replied. "Go ahead."

"OK. Aunt Edith. I mean, Edith… can you first explain to me why you call my mom Pelican and why she refers to you as Trident?"

"Ha. Yes. That's kind of a funny one. As you know, your mom is from Louisiana, whose state bird is the pelican."

"Oh. So that much is true." Anna rolled her eyes.

"Why would we lie about that?" Edith asked.

"Why indeed! Never mind. Continue."

"OK. As I said, your mom is from Louisiana, and if you've ever watched a pelican as she sits peacefully on the surface of the ocean, she can perceive what no one else can, all the fish swimming unheedingly underneath her. When she decides it's time for a meal, she takes to the air, dives suddenly under the water, and effortlessly snags her target."

"Yes. I've seen that," Anna said. "That makes sense. But where did you get your name, Trident?"

"If you've watched that pelican carefully, you've seen the shape she takes on as she's diving. Her wings are folded back into sharp points on both sides of her body, and her feet are pointed straight back in between the wings. As her body pierces the surface of the water, she takes on a form that looks just like a trident."

Anna thought about the birds she had watched with such enjoyment while relaxing on the beach. She understood that what Edith said about the form the diving pelican took on was quite descriptive of a trident. "But why do they call *you* Trident?"

"Because the trident follows the pelican. It gives her the form and the force she needs to make the kills. Without the trident, the pelican would starve. This is why I was so angry with you when you didn't call me when your mom had such difficulties. It was a couple of years since her diagnosis, and I thought you had everything under control."

"You don't know the shame I felt after all the slander Mama spread about me," Anna cried. "I didn't want to tell anyone about our business after that."

"Anna, you should have contacted Pierce anyway. He was continuously in contact with me. I was trying to separate myself from my former occupation. It was time. I'm getting on in age so all I wanted to do was relax in my remaining years. Your thoughtless actions have ruined all that. Thank you very much!"

"Number one, I don't contact Pierce — ever! You made me think he was my cousin, so when I fell in love with him, I felt like an incestuous perv!"

"What? Wait! You fell in love with Pierce? How did I not know that?"

"Well, I don't know, Edith. I thought you knew everything. I don't know how you didn't know that too. Thank you very much for ruining our lives!"

"Why didn't Pierce tell me?"

"Who knows? I guess you'll have to ask him. He is your son, isn't he? Or maybe that's a lie too."

Mama had been sitting there quietly while all this went on. Then she began laughing and said, "Ha! Edith. I guess all that chiding you gave me about sheltering my daughter has come back to bite you. Now who did the sheltering? Ha, ha, ha, ha! Now that you two have cleared the air, let's get on with the mission. Who are we shadowing? Did you get the recipe from the magazine? I didn't get my cooking magazine in the mail because my know-it-all daughter moved me into that home. Thanks for busting me out, Edith. So, Anna's an operative too now? I won't abide the organization making her kill though. She has to be backup only. Oh, you don't know how bored I've been! Let's get to it!"

Chapter Nine

"Pelican, dear," Edith began, "I don't think you appreciate what's going on here. We aren't *on* a mission; we *are* the mission."

"I don't understand! Why is everyone constantly treating me like I don't know what's going on? My daughter told that doctor to say I have Alzheimer's just so she can take my money. How's that for gratitude toward a devoted mother? Now you think I don't know what's going on? Well, I do know what's going on. You're my partner. We have been given a target. My daughter has decided to finally do something meaningful with her life and quit that nowhere job she had fixing up other people's houses. Glad to have you on-board, Anna. Now — that's what's going on!"

"I hate to break this to you, Pelican, but we aren't after a target. We are the target."

Mama's mouth dropped open and she had nothing else to say.

Anna leaned forward and explained. "Mama, apparently, I was mistaken sending you to that nursing home. I was so afraid when you began getting lost and asking strangers for help, that I thought I was doing the

44

right thing to protect you. I've never taken any money from you. All I've done is try to help you. I didn't know I was actually putting you into danger."

"Yes, Pelican. I got the recipe in my online subscription to The Cooking School. They're doing everything electronically now, dear. You weren't able to keep up. I understand that. It's why you were printing out your files rather than keeping them password protected on your computer. That was a very dangerous thing to do, Pelican.

"The recipe for the cooked goose was sent out. I couldn't, wouldn't follow that recipe. Even though we're not genetically sisters, I love you like a sister. I could never terminate you. I knew I had to save you.

"Even though Pierce is management, he understands. He's going to help us, that is, if we can get to him in time. Keep a sharp eye out. I'm a bit concerned that they might follow my carefully hidden escape route and catch up with us before we can get you safely hidden away."

Anna looked out the van window and saw that they were crossing the Lake Pontchartrain Bridge. This twenty-four-mile-long bridge led right into New Orleans. They were sitting ducks for the full length of the crossing. Aunt Edith, while spry for her age, was no match for any type of confrontation, and Mama could no longer walk even with the aid of her wheeled walker. She had begun to shuffle her feet at a snail's pace. Anna had had to quit checking her out of the nursing home because it seemed that every time she did Mama managed to take a tumble at the slightest crack in the sidewalk. The last time had left her with a broken wrist, so she couldn't even brace herself on her walker any more. She had lost so much strength that even her poor ambulatory skills had deserted her. She was only able to get around in a wheelchair now, and not very effectively at that.

Anna looked behind her into the back of the van to make sure she could locate the chair. There it was by the back door. That knowledge could come in handy in a tight situation.

Anna thought about how long it had been since she had been on the bridge. How old was she? Eighteen? Probably the trip she took with friends after high school. New Orleans was sort of a rite of passage for high schoolers in south Louisiana. It no longer held charm for her. She was glad that she had left her home state and gone to college at Indiana University in Bloomington. It made everything from her youth seem like it was someone else's life.

After her brief marriage and divorce, she had thrown herself into her work. Some wouldn't find it very glamorous, but she loved it. She would buy an old broken-down house that she could still discover the charm underneath, make sure the roofing joists and foundation were sound, explore the neighborhood and decide if a middle-income family would enjoy it, do the creative work required to make it a home, and then sell it to a family who would love it.

Anna used to daydream about the happy families who made her renovated houses into their homes. Their children would grow up with a security that attached itself to their family, their house, their neighborhood, their school and their church. It was the American dream, and Anna made sure she helped some people to enjoy it, even though she never had.

But then she started getting the disjointed phone calls from Mama. Sometimes she was perfectly coherent, and then other times she couldn't string together an intelligible sentence.

Mama wouldn't admit to Anna that she was having financial difficulties, so she went to Edith. Finally, it became too much for even her dear friend. Edith knew that Anna would come to the rescue when she was called. For some reason, it was always Anna who couldn't turn away someone, especially family, in need.

She chose her husband because she could see he needed her. All her life, she wanted to be needed, until she came to the conclusion that she was just being used. Mama never spoke a word of gratitude for the fact that Anna had left her home and business behind in Indiana when she came back to a state that held no pleasant memories for her in order to become her caregiver. Anna had a strong sense of duty, so she would do it anyway. But a tiny show of gratitude would be so appreciated.

From her place in the backseat, Anna could see the frown on Edith's face, as she kept glancing into the rearview mirror. "What's wrong, Edith? Are you worried that EMS will want their body back that you blew up in mama's trailer?"

"No. I don't expect any problems with that. I waited until the morgue arrived to take the dear departed away from the home before I pulled the fire alarm. They were in the middle of loading the body when they left it behind in order to help with the emergency — save the living instead of the dead and all that. I tossed the body into the van and rolled your mom out the door in the midst of the panic. If they're smart, they'll cover their own asses. Oops! Sorry Anna.

"Anyway, have you ever seen a panic at a nursing home? It's impossible to hurry up the elderly and demented. It would have been funny had it not been so pathetic, but it gave us exactly what we required. Now all we need is for that suspicious car that's been following us to come around and get on their way so my stomach can settle. You don't have any antacids in your purse, do you?"

"Yes. I think I do. Edith, that body — you didn't hurry the old lady to a convenient grave, did you?"

"My goodness, girl! What do you take me for? I don't kill innocent people, especially such helpless people. No. I'd known this dear lady was on her way to glory for a couple of days. I just waited until the opportune moment. I did hope she didn't delay too long since we were up against a deadline."

"Deadline?"

"Yes. Literally. When the order went out to make sure your mom couldn't reveal secrets, I was the closest. Even though I've been retired, I still stay in the loop."

"I'm glad you were there, Edith. I had no idea. Sorry."

Mama spoke up and said, "I'm glad you two think you can... um... con... collu... oh, what's the word? You didn't include me. I can decide things for myself. Let me off. I'm walking."

Chapter Ten

Pierce finished putting the signs on the front and back doors and sending all the workers away with the promise of compensation for lost work. "Go out! Have fun! Listen to some street musicians! I'll be in touch." He scanned the area and then crossed to the parking garage where he paid an exorbitant monthly fee to park his beige Camry. One thing he had learned early in this job — never stand out. His car was as forgettable as his clothing and hairstyle. Middle American male — nothing special.

He pulled out of the garage and began a circuitous route to the church building. Whoever might be looking for him would be people he knew, maybe even some he had trained, unless they brought in the foreign element.

The Cooking School was an international organization that used mercenaries from various nations. Those could be quite unpredictable and sometimes too ruthless, but the current world political situation occasionally required extreme measures. Pierce understood that death was a part of life, and more frequently than he preferred, a part necessary in order to allow innocent people to live their lives in relative peace.

He couldn't imagine having any other career. He got to pair his two passions — food and freedom.

The Cooking School was the perfect cover for the troubling part of the government that was tasked with taking care of the kind of business most people would consider heinous. Yes, killing was heinous, but he knew that even more killing would occur if they didn't carry out their strategic strikes. He was horrified when he first learned that his own mother was a trained assassin. What young man wouldn't be? But when he considered the occupation he imagined she was engaged in, he found it the superior choice. Pierce had spent his formative years thinking his mom was a prostitute, and to him, killing was preferable to prostitution. Working for the organization to keep the nation safe was noble. Being a prostitute was... something else.

In the early days, The Cooking School used recipes in women's magazines to communicate operations to the agents. This was why his mom and Anna's mom always had piles of women's magazines around. Some of them communicated pertinent information, and some were just used as cover to divert attention from the essential.

Neither his mom nor Anna's ever seemed to have much real interest in following all those beautifully illustrated recipes to whip up appetizing family dinners. They had discussed this as children, and bore some resentment toward the whole thing. Pierce began following the recipes and enjoyed creating amazing meals for his mom when she returned home from her various forays. Anna, instead, fell in love with the beautiful houses and the rooms depicted in the magazines. She lived out fantasies in childhood that she caused to become realities in adulthood. Both Anna and Pierce pursued careers that were inspired indirectly by their mothers' occupations.

Pierce perfected the use of communication through recipes and started using the online forum to handle the agents in the field. He used his restaurant not only as a cover for his interest in cooking and creating masterpieces of cuisine, it was his inspiration. In the process of training new recruits, he also taught them to cook. They developed relationships that went beyond their profession through the medium of good food. He was thinking of how he would greet Trident, Pelican and Anna when they arrived. He decided that a stop off at the market would be necessary. He had access to the large kitchen in the fellowship hall of the church to prepare the meal.

***

He let himself in through the back foyer of the church with his arms full of groceries. Since his mom had called that morning and told him that he would be seeing them that evening, he had been continuously bustling with arrangements. Now it was time to handle the preparation he preferred — that of creating exquisite cuisine.

He started chopping onions, garlic and bell pepper. Then he cut up the large roast and sliced the andouille sausage. He sautéed the vegetables in bacon fat while he prepared the dark roux with real grass-fed butter and unbleached flour. In another large iron skillet, he quick-seared the pieces of roast and added the sliced andouille. He then combined the three pots into one and added some beef broth and Ro Tel tomatoes. Now it was time to let the pot simmer for a couple of hours. When ready to serve, he would boil one pot of brown rice for forty-five minutes and one pot of basmati rice for twenty minutes. He would then combine them and cook for about five more minutes until they would stick together.

When he served his delectable dish, he would use a shallow bowl for the stew portion and place a round lump of sticky rice in the middle with a sprinkling of chopped cilantro on top. Pierce had a zeal for making his food present well. It was part of the experience, and after the day he knew his loved ones must have endured, this would be just what they needed. *Loved ones!* Did he truly think that word? He had to admit to himself that he did.

Chapter Eleven

Anna knew that the best way to deal with Mama was to placate her and make her think she was getting what she wanted. "Where are you going to walk to, Mama? You can't go. We need you. You see that olive-green Charger back there? We think he's following us. What do you think?"

Mama had had a spinal fusion in her neck a few years prior, so she couldn't turn to look back. "I can't see anything back there. I guess you'll have to saw... er... place... oh, what do I mean to say?" She was getting frustrated with her inability to express herself. The stress was making the symptoms worse.

"Don't worry about it, Mama. You've got me on the team now. I'll keep an eye out." About that time, the car sped up and went around them as they were passing the Super Dome on the elevated freeway. Anna let out a sigh of relief. "How much further to the restaurant, Edith?"

"Almost there. I haven't been able to check to see if Pierce has tried to contact us, so I assume everything is the same. He should be in the kitchen; we'll just pull around to the back." Up ahead, Edith saw the green Charger barely concealed in an alley. Anna had already jumped to the pavement, gotten the wheelchair out, and was unloading Pelican into it. "Look out!" Edith bellowed. Four men were approaching from the alley.

"Let me at 'em!" Mama shrieked. Without warning, she kicked out her feet and pulled the chair out of Anna's grasp. The momentum of the slight decline in the road kept her going. She was screeching in an unearthly tone. The young men were startled and alarmed at the apparition careening toward them with her white hair flying and her feet stuck out in front of her. "My voodoo is after you! You will all die, die, die!" Mama screamed at the top of her lungs.

Three of the men turned and ran but one stood his ground. As Mama approached, he reached out and stopped her chair. "Hi, little granny. You're going to get hurt like that," he said, holding onto her wheelchair. "You remind me of my little granny. Now what's all this talk about voodoo?"

"You let go of me, you young hoodlum. Do you know who I am? I am the most dangerous woman you have ever met. If you don't let go and get out of my path, you will feel the full fury of my wrath land on your head. You hear me!"

The young man began to laugh heartily; his three associates turned at the sound and walked back to the ridiculous scene playing out in the alleyway. "Listen, Granny. Let me introduce myself. My name is Alexandro. Do you know how much danger you're in? You've been saying a lot of things you shouldn't, and there are a couple more teams out looking for you. The order is to silence you one way or another. Do you know what that means?"

Mama's mouth formed a small 'o' for a moment as she struggled to comprehend. Her eyes darted back and forth in confusion. Light was dawning on her understanding. "Oh my! This is serious!"

"Yes, Granny, it is. Now what are we going to do about it?"

Edith walked up and put out her hand. "Hello, Alexandro. I've heard of you, but I've never had the pleasure of meeting you. I'm Trident."

Alexandro presented a serious salute. "I'm most honored to meet you, Trident."

"Thank you. Do you know who this little old lady is?"

"Who are you calling old?" Mama said as she struggled to try to stand up from her chair.

"Sit down, Mama," Anna said as she trotted up to join the conversation. "You are Pelican! You don't need to stand for anyone!" She knew that she had to appeal to Mama's vanity because, if she tried to say she couldn't stand up, it would only make her angry and more determined to try.

"Pelican! My great pleasure!" Alexandro saluted her as well. The only name we were given was—"

"That's OK!" stated Edith. "You know who she is now."

"Now what are we going to do about our little problem?" asked Alexandro.

"We have no problem. I'm on a mission. Now you and your boys back away and let me get on with my work," Mama stated in a most authoritative way.

"Pelican," Edith said, "Alexandro and I must have a little 'need to know' conversation." She draped her arm over Alexandro's shoulders and sauntered away with him. He was nodding his head vigorously and shook hands when they were finished. Then he gathered up his team and walked back to Mama where he bowed and kissed the back of her hand. He knew exactly how to charm the ladies. All three of them let out a big sigh as he drove away.

"The parking lot is empty," Edith observed. Then she detected the sign on the back door. "Uh oh. I'd better check this out."

"I'll come with you. Mama, sit here and catch your breath for a minute after all the excitement. We'll be back as soon as we see where Pierce is, OK?" Mama waited in her wheelchair next to the van door. Anna made sure to firmly lock the wheels.

"Don't let her out of your sight," Edith said.

"I've got my eye on her. Edith, why did the men leave?"

"I assured them that I had Pelican under control and would make sure she didn't talk to anyone."

"So, we're safe now?"

"I only wish. The other teams might not have a sweet little granny they love. When there's money involved, you can't trust anyone. The next group might be, in fact probably will be, more aggressive. I hear they're from Canada."

"Is that bad?" asked Anne.

"It is not only bad, it's terrible. They feel like they have something to prove. We'd best be very, very careful. Anyway, this note says the restaurant is closed. I need to check The Cooking School website. I'm sure he left us some breadcrumbs there."

Anna helped Mama settle back into the van. It was a lot more trouble getting her in than out. Mama was shaped like a little apple. She had always been slight of build, but her inactivity in recent years had changed her figure. She had lost height from her osteoporosis, and gained girth from her sedentary lifestyle. The Alzheimer's disease caused her motor skills to be more and more unreliable as her brain deteriorated in countless ways.

Anna braced her feet wide apart and gently lifted and guided Mama to help support her into a standing position. Then, she got behind her and gave her the extra lift she would need to step up onto the runner beside the van and then turn quickly to plop into the seat. Anna then buckled her in, wondering how they would manage in another emergency situation.

Edith eased back into the driver's seat as Anna was getting buckled up in the back. "Where is he?"

"He's at the church," Edith answered.

"How did you figure that out?"

"Well, what would you think if you saw the notice was for recipes for a church social?" Edith smiled.

"The only one who would know where to go would be someone with inside knowledge, Edith. Are you the only one who has that?"

"I think so… I hope so."

Chapter Twelve

Pierce opened the company website to see if his message had been received. There it was — the thumbs up emoji from Trident. Good. That meant they were on their way.

Pierce scanned the site carefully to make sure there were no intruders checking up too. The article was in Cajun French, so that meant not many people would be able to easily understand it. Maybe just French Canadians or Haitians, who both spoke a vernacular French that was similar to the Cajun. That limited the field so much that he felt reasonably safe.

He heard a furtive creaking sound above him on the ground floor. It was probably the arrival of his guests. He was looking forward to seeing his mom, but his heart skipped a beat at knowing he would be seeing Anna again. "I'm down here in the kitchen," he called out.

"That's good to know" said the stranger flanked by two very serious looking fellows.

Pierce instinctively picked up the boiling pot of sauce piquant and threw it toward the men. The closest one was drenched with the steaming stew and began screaming. He licked his burning arm and yelled, "Ow, ow, ow — oh tellement délicieux! Ow! Ow! Ow! But it burns! But oh my! So delicious!"

Pierce quickly ducked out the back door of the kitchen area that led to a small Sunday school classroom. He pressed a button hidden in a groove of the door jamb that lifted the street-level window and the bars on the outside of it. He leaped on a table top and then plunged himself out of the window and onto the sidewalk.

He barely made it through before the timer he had rigged on the window and the bars slammed shut. He was rolling toward the street when he caught himself, jumped to his feet and into a full run without missing a beat. Even though he was a chef and tasted all his creations, he made sure to moderate his eating and to spend all his extra time keeping his body fit for just such an emergency.

He ran across the now dark intersection to an adjacent group of buildings while using his phone trying to send out an alert to the women. He plunged down the staircase cleverly concealed by a pair of dumpsters just as the two unscathed men emerged from the church.

They had ordered the man impaired by boiling sauce piquant to stay behind to wait for the arrival of their target. They looked up and down the street and surmised there was no way Pierce could have run far enough in either direction to have made it outside their field of vision yet. They began searching in every conceivable nook and cranny.

Pierce sprinted through the basement of the building and came to the adjacent brick wall. He flipped the hidden lever and passed through the door. At this point, he was in a tunnel connected to the next building. He entered the building and ran up the stairs to the roof. He pulled out his key to open the door and then made sure it was latched behind him. He then walked toward a dummy air duct and pulled out the go-bag he had hoped never to need. It contained, among various necessary items, a pair of binoculars.

From a concealed opening in the roof enclosure, Pierce looked out, hoping that his mom and guests wouldn't be arriving. Sadly, within seconds, he saw the van pull up. He watched Anna emerge from the side door and then head to the back of the van where she pulled out a wheelchair.

Though twenty years had passed, at least from this distance, she hadn't changed a bit. He could see her golden-brown hair glowing under the light of the streetlamp. Her figure was still lithe and graceful. He swallowed the lump in his throat at the same time his heart was racing in panic for their safety. He knew that if he dashed down among them now, they would all be in greater danger. He would just have to trust in the care and professionalism of Trident. Though he wasn't known for praying much, he figured that this was the perfect time to give it a try. Anna would appreciate it.

He was on the verge of panic when he heard the gunshot, but then, his prayers were answered. No more than five minutes after entering the building, all three of them were back at the van loading up. He watched them squeal out of the parking lot while he observed helplessly. They were so close, and then, just like that, they were out of his grasp. He would pull out all the stops and use his last resource to regain them.

Chapter Thirteen

Anna couldn't wait to see Pierce again, but she was also nervous about it. What if he had a special someone in his life? Surely, he no longer felt the same about her, especially since he knew they weren't cousins long before she did. He had never tried to contact her or renew their relationship. She would just play it cool, aloof even. They were all in danger and needed sharp wits. A silly romance would be a distraction they didn't need right now. For all her self-talk, nothing could take those butterflies out of her stomach as they approached the handicapped entrance to the church.

She was getting accustomed to loading and unloading Mama from the van. They were quickly, at least for them, concluding the short walk to the lighted entryway. Edith led the way and was using precautions with her approach. One could never be too careful, was what she always said. Once inside, they started to push Mama's chair to the small elevator that would take them to the basement floor.

Mama refused to get on the elevator. "No way I'm getting into that box! I'll just stay up here."

"Mama," Anna sighed. "Pierce has prepared a meal for us and we're all going to go down and sit around a table together. It's been a long day. I'm just not up to this."

"Just push me over into that dark corner by the stairs, and you two go on down. Trust me. I know what I'm doing." As they passed by the front door, Mama snagged an umbrella out of the stand by the main entrance. When she settled into her safe place, she opened it up.

It looked like someone had just tossed their umbrella onto a wheelchair. The Afghan that covered Mama's legs and feet appeared as if it had been haphazardly crumpled there as well. As usual, Mama had a way of making any place she landed look cluttered and unplanned.

Anna gave a harrumph of exasperation. That was Mama. What could she do?

Edith preceded Anna down the stars only slightly ahead of her. The man at the bottom was wet with something that looked painful, which covered his obviously burned arms and chest. He had a gun pointed straight at them and a huge arrogant grin on his face. "Glad to see you finally showed up."

Edith jumped in front of Anna as the boom of the gun bounced off the cement walls of the basement making the sound bound around the room, impossibly loud. She turned and shoved the younger woman ahead of her, and they scrambled back up the stairs.

Anna was wondering frantically how she would ever get her mama out of that church. They ran past her in the dark before they perceived it. The man charging up the stairs didn't notice her either until an open umbrella was shoved into his face. In his shock, he jumped back and fell down the hazardous cement staircase. Edith and Anna turned around to grab Mama and glanced at the man sprawled awkwardly at the bottom. His crumpled, shattered body gave evidence that he hadn't survived the fall.

Back outside, Edith and Anna practically dumped Mama back into her seat. Anna didn't bother carefully placing the wheelchair in the back but just pushed the sidearms together and shoved it ahead of her through the sliding door just as Edith was peeling out of the handicapped parking space. Anna bounced around in the back before she was able to struggle into her seat and buckle up. "Where to now?" she shouted.

"Guess," yelled Edith.

"I don't know!

"Neither do I."

Mama just smiled. "Maybe we ought to find a doctor for that shoulder there, Trident."

"What?" Edith looked down and saw that she had been hit. In the shock of the situation, she hadn't even felt it.

Chapter Fourteen

Pierce watched the two men poke around the area until they decided to go back inside. He could clearly hear them speaking French as they agreed to pick up his trail later. They were going to try to catch the women, not realizing that the women had come and gone while they had conducted their fruitless search. The sound of the gunshot didn't register any alarms in their minds because this neighborhood was known for abundant gang activity.

A few minutes later, they re-emerged from the building carrying their injured or dead partner. Pierce couldn't tell which. The way they were shouting and handling the man so carelessly suggested that he was beyond medical remediation. They shoved the body into the trunk, which made the guess a certainty, and then squealed out of the parking lot on the side of the building opposite to where the three women had peeled out only moments before. Pierce couldn't imagine what had happened, but he knew he now had some very angry Canadians on his hands.

Pierce went back into the building and walked through some maze-like passages before making his cautious exit two blocks behind the Camp Street church. He walked a few miles through the dark city until he saw the homeless shelter up ahead. Pierce knew his demeanor was that of someone down on his luck. He would fit right in.

"Do you have any beds for tonight?" he asked the kind looking man. "I'm out of work and thought I would have a new job by today, but it fell through. I don't have anywhere else to go."

"I have a few beds available as long as you're sober and not on the run from the police."

"I'm good on both those accounts."

"OK. Let me collect a little information about you: name, next of kin, age, profession and last address. Then just sign the book and we'll get you settled."

Everything Pierce wrote down was false except for his profession. When the social worker read over his information, his eyebrows went up when he saw that Pierce was a cook. He didn't use the word chef, that would seem presumptuous in this setting, but 'cook' should get him a little appreciation if the people were hungry.

"Cook, huh? Do you have a specialty?

"What else? Cajun and Creole," Pierce answered.

"Well, Joe," this was Pierce's chosen pseudonym, "it looks like your arrival was right on time. Let me introduce myself," he said sticking out his hand. "I'm Todd. I've been having to do the cooking, and everyone calls me kitchen impaired. I know you can't be worse than I am."

"I hope I can provide a satisfactory breakfast tomorrow morning. Right now, I'm pretty beat and would like to get settled in."

"Sure thing, Joe. Follow me. I'll get you taken care of."

They walked through a casual, comfortable looking living room with mismatched furniture and a giant TV screen. Men were sitting around talking and laughing. It didn't look like anyone was watching the news that featured a typically striking, young, blonde reporter standing in front of a large brick structure on Camp Street.

"If you look behind me," she gestured, "you will see what looks like a peaceful setting, an old, beautiful church building, but the reports of gunshots and the smear of blood that have been found at the bottom of the basement stairs tell a different story. Right now, it's all a mystery, but we'll keep you up to date as the facts come in. Now, back to you, Richard."

Chapter Fifteen

€dith pulled the van off on the side of the road. "There's a first aid kit in the back there. Look around. It's the box with the big red X on it."

"Your injury hasn't impaired your sarcasm, Aunt Edith."

"I thought I told you I'm not your aunt."

"Sorry. Force of habit. You still feel like my aunt."

Anna found the box and opened it up. She saw some betadine and a roll of gauze. She squatted behind Edith and fumbled with the supplies. She wasn't very good with this sort of thing but somehow managed to suppress her desire to gag. She knew enough to pour the betadine on the wound and then to wrap it firmly with the sterile gauze she took out of the sealed package. "That should do you for a while, but you certainly require more treatment than this. We need to get you to a doctor."

"I can't trust stopping in this city. I need someone we can confide in," Edith said. "Anna, you're going to have to drive."

"Here, Edith. I can help you," Anna said as Edith struggled to get out of the van.

"I don't need any help. It's just a scratch." Edith opened the driver's door and tried to climb out. "Ooooo. Well, I wasn't expecting that!" She bent her head over and laid it on the seat. "I guess I'm not as young as I used to be. Maybe a little help would be appreciated."

Anna gently walked Edith around the van and removed the wheelchair that was still in the way. After stowing it properly, she helped Edith get comfortable in the back seat. "I don't mind driving at all, but where can we find a doctor who won't report us to the authorities?"

Mama spoke up. "Just get back on Interstate twelve and head north. I know where we can get some help. It will take about an hour. Can you make it that long… um… uh… who are you again?"

"Oh, dear!" Anna breathed out. She did as she was told, but didn't know where it would lead. She knew that they would be in Baton Rouge in about an hour, but what then?

Chapter Sixteen

Pierce was rooting around in the pantry and refrigerator looking for ingredients for breakfast for twenty men. There were eggs, thankfully, and lots of cans of spam. He was pleased to find onions and Velveeta cheese. Not exactly what he would have chosen. He was glad he had called himself a cook instead of a chef. Digging through the refrigerator, he was delighted to come across some big, one-pound packs of real butter. *Now we're cooking!*

There were flour and baking powder too. With those ingredients, and a little sugar and salt, breakfast would be complete.

He measured everything into a large bowl to mix together all the dry products. Then, he cut the cold butter up into chunks and got his hands into the mixture to work the butter into the dry ingredients until it was the perfect consistency. He added some canned milk, another sad concession to buttermilk, and rolled the dough out. There wasn't a biscuit cutter, but a glass from the overhead cabinet worked just fine. He was well-known for his homemade biscuits. The oven was preheated to the optimum biscuit-cooking temperature of 450 degrees. Ten minutes later, the fluffy, lightly browned biscuits were hot and perfect. The spam, onions and Velveeta were chopped and ready to throw into the omelets as the men smelled the biscuits and began arriving in the kitchen. 'Joe' became the most popular man in the shelter.

A different social worker showed up from the one Pierce had met the night before. "I hear we finally have someone who can cook around here. My name's Michael. Glad to meet you." Michael stuck out his hand.

Pierce wiped his hands on his jeans as a precaution from any remaining ingredients and reciprocated the friendly offering.

"Ha. Sorry we don't have no aprons for ya'. No chef hats either."

"That's quite all right. I know how to make do. Would you like for me to whip up an omelet for you?"

"I would appreciate it, but my wife made me eat a bowl full of some kind of cereal that's supposed to be good for me. It tasted like the box it was packed in, but…" Michael looked down at his portly frame. "I guess she's right. Between her and the doctor, I don't know who I'm more afraid of." Michael let out a hearty laugh. "You know, Joe, Todd called me this morning about you. He said that if your cooking's any good, we might have a few funds to pay you a little something if you'd be willing to stick around a while. It would really help us out if we can keep these men fed so we don't have a mutiny on our hands. Is the food any good?" Michael called out.

Men with mouths full yelled unintelligible sounds of appreciation.

"Well, job interview over! Would you like to help us? I know you're looking for a real job, but in the meantime, you could stay here. It would be a roof over your head and free meals. What do you say?"

Pierce appreciated that the homeless shelter would be a good place for him to land while he was trying to figure out how to save Pelican and reconnect with Anna. He knew he was taking his mom for granted in the concoction he was brewing, but that's what mothers are for, right? He would require access to a computer. There were some people he needed to find and some others he had to try to solicit help from.

"If there is a public library close by, I could use that to aid with my job search. I don't have transportation right now, so it's important for me to be able to reach out."

"Oh! No problem," Michael said. "We have a library about a mile up the road. You look fit enough to walk there. Will that suffice?"

"That should work." Pierce smiled. "You've got a deal." This time it was Pierce sticking his hand out first.

Chapter Seventeen

It was the middle of the night as they entered the outskirts of Baton Rouge. Anna reached across the console to poke Mama awake. She tried repeatedly with no success. She looked behind her at Edith and saw that she was asleep too. Anna exited the interstate and drove down the highway looking for a place to pull over. She saw a large church building on the right — Sherwood Forest Baptist Church. She took the van around to the back of the huge building and parked in the vast parking lot behind a row of azalea bushes. This would have to do until morning. She cracked the windows down about an inch all around to provide a little ventilation, and then she shut off the engine. Anna was finally able to lean her seat back and fall into an exhausted, though restless, sleep.

She knew how much she needed her sleep, but her night visions were filled with various people chasing after her. She dreamed that Mama and Edith were little babies wrapped in the kinds of blankets they use in the neonatal unit of the hospital. She kept trying to find a safe place to put the babies, but she was never able to outrun the faceless ones chasing her.

Her chest hurt with the pain of the memory of a baby lost somewhere in a preemie unit over ten years ago. She was struggling in her dreams and finally jerked awake. The sky was just beginning to turn pink in the east, and Mama was staring at her with an expression Anna had never seen on her before. She looked down and saw that her mother had wet herself. It dawned on her that she was completely unprepared for this. Her mama needed some adult diapers.

"Oh no," she answered. "I'm sorry, Mama. We're going to have to go find a drug store. Then how about we go to McDonald's where you can change and we can get some breakfast?" Her own bladder was causing her some discomfort too, so she knew that all their needs would require prompt attention.

Mama's face lit up like a child's. Also like a child, she loved McDonald's. Anna was glad that in the midst of the danger and chaos, she could do something to make Mama happy.

"What's going on?" Edith groaned from the back seat. "Oooooo. Well, that little gunshot wound sure has gotten uncomfortable. It doesn't look like it's bleeding through the bandage though, so I think I'm good for a while"

"I'm so sorry, Edith. We're going to a drug store for some Depends, and then we're going to McDonald's for breakfast. We'll feel better if we can get a little shot of grease and caffeine to start our morning. We'll get you to a doctor right after that, I promise." Anna worried that she was lying to Edith, but she was going to take care of one

76

crisis at a time, and right now, bathroom needs and food came first.

There was a locally owned pharmacy kitty-corner across from the McDonald's. Anna jumped out of the van and ran in as Mama sat there looking longingly at the McDonald's restaurant. Walking up to the counter, Anna asked the pharmacist if she could buy a suture kit. To her surprise, he sold it to her without any problem. "You got a farm?" he asked.

"Um, yes," she answered, figuring it was the easiest solution. "Horse cut himself up on the barbed wire fence."

"Happens all the time," he said with a smile.

As soon as Anna climbed back into the van after only about five minutes, Mama said, "I'm hungry. There's a McDonald's. We're going to eat, aren't we?"

"Of course we are!" Anna exclaimed. "I told you we're going to McDonald's, remember?"

"You did not! You never tell me what's going on. You act like you think you're the mama. I'm the mama! Now, take me to that McDonald's right there!" she shouted, pointing out the window.

"Yes, Mama," Anna replied meekly.

Mama was placated and smiled expectantly as they pulled into the parking lot. Anna grabbed a Depends out of the package and put it into her large bag. Then she ran around to the back and took out the wheelchair. As she pulled it to the passenger side, Edith was struggling to get down through the back-sliding door. Her face was pale and Anna could see that she was having trouble. "Hold tight until I get Mama seated and then you can lean on me to get into the restaurant."

It was a challenge to get the two impaired women through the door. The tension bar kept trying to close on them as they worked their way through. "Now I see why handicapped doors are so important!" Anna said. "They have a ramp here but no button to hold open the door. Who designs these things?"

She wasn't expecting an answer from her exhausted companions, but Mama said, "I don't know. Why are you asking me?" Anna just rolled her eyes... again.

Edith managed to get through the door to the ladies' room while Anna pushed Mama's wheelchair into the family restroom. *Thank goodness for whoever came up with these!*

There were plenty of paper towels and lots of nice, warm soapy water. She washed Mama off and helped change the Depends. Then, she dried her pants as much as possible under the hand dryer. Mama looked at her with an expression Anna had never seen. Something very clear and beautiful filled Mama's pale blue eyes. Then she said, "I love you."

Anna struggled to push back the tears as she briskly finished helping Mama dress and get back into the chair. Then she hurriedly gave herself a little sponge-down too.

She had sometimes wondered how homeless people managed. It was something she never thought she would have found out first hand, and for some reason, she was becoming emotionally overwhelmed. Maybe just a filling meal and a little rest. Yes. That's all she needed.

Chapter Eighteen

Pierce was walking back to the homeless shelter after several hours of research at the library. He was thankful for the foresight to include the fake identity papers in his emergency go-bag. If anyone saw the search done by Joseph Bryan, it wouldn't send up any red flags. He was just Joe B. Citizen expressing his interest.

He was curious about various cooking schools around the world, including Canada, Mexico, Haiti, Belize and Argentina. He left out those on the other side of the world. He didn't think they would activate for this little problem. Haiti and Belize weren't terribly far from New Orleans if one had the correct transportation. He left hidden messages in the websites of the Haiti and Belize schools. Maybe someone could help inject some common sense into this big mess he and his loved ones found themselves in.

There was that expression again… loved ones. Pierce mentally acknowledged the truth of the statement — for all three of the ladies. He knew they were smart, strong and independent, though the years had gotten the better of two of them, but he couldn't just sit back and expect this to turn out all right without his help.

He picked up his pace. The shelter provided breakfast and supper, and he was responsible for the nutritional well-being of twenty men who were depending on him. There was a lot of work to do to figure out how to cook a desirable meal with the hodgepodge of ingredients the charitable food pantry sporadically supplied.

His mind was churning vigorously between what to fix for supper and what he would do to help save the most important people in his life. Besides, he had given the murderous group from the church last night the slip thoroughly enough that he thought there was no way they could catch up to him any time soon. His unit had run so smoothly for him for the past several years, that he must have been losing his edge. These were his last thoughts as the black bag went over his head and he felt the dreaded prick of the needle in his neck.

Chapter Nineteen

After watching the news last night, Pastor Davis thought he was prepared for the knock on his door. In fact, he was surprised it hadn't come sooner. Peering through the lace curtain confirmed his fears, and he swallowed the lump he felt forming in his aging gullet. His wrinkled neck was still trembling and the tendons were still bulging with his effort. He cleared his throat as he opened the door. "Yes, detectives? What can I do for you?"

"May we come in, sir?" The younger detective looked stern and a bit arrogant, while the older one looked contrite and apologetic.

"Of course, young men, you are welcome into my home," the octogenarian pastor said as they walked past him. "Can I get you a cool drink? The missus isn't well, but she always makes sure we keep something on hand for guests."

"We aren't guests." The younger detective spoke again. "We're here on official business. "I don't suppose you watched the news last night?"

The pastor hung his head. "I'm sad to say that I did."

This time the older detective spoke up. "Pastor Davis, my name is Detective MacGregor, and this is Detective

Brown. We aren't accusing you of anything, we'd just like to get any information that could shed light on the mystery of the blood on the floor of your church. It didn't appear there was forced entry, but with the report of the gunshot and the… other evidence… left behind, there was probably something going on there that you had no part in, though you might know of someone who does. Any little thing you can tell us will help."

"I'm sorry, son." Detective MacGregor smiled slightly at being referred to as son, especially since he was nearing retirement. "I wish I could help you."

"Well, Pastor, we've been looking into the church's finances and have found some rather unusual bank deposits. What can you tell us about that?"

Pastor Davis' eyebrows went up. "Do you think there could be any connection?" He couldn't keep the quiver out of his voice, ravaged as it was, from many years of delivering fiery sermons. "We have an anonymous donor. Without him we wouldn't be able to keep the church doors open. All he asks is for the occasional use of the building. I've always suspected that maybe he's trying to help people get off drugs, and he needs a safe place for them to work through their issues. Do you think it's possible that someone was playing around with a gun and was injured? I surely hope not."

"If that were the case, they would have shown up at a hospital. New Orleans hospitals get their fair share of gunshot injuries, but the locations and circumstances of all those reported last night indicate they could not have been from your church," MacGregor explained.

"Tell us what you know!" Brown snapped. "We can do it here or downtown. Your choice!"

At this point, the pastor's breathing was becoming labored. A tiny, frail lady clutching a walker appeared in the doorway. "What is going on? Don, are you OK? What are you doing to my husband?" Mrs Davis struggled into the room. The indignation her frail frame imparted, with her shoulders thrown back in spite of her bent figure, intimidated both of the detectives. They jumped to their feet and began apologizing.

"I'm sure this is all just a misunderstanding. Pastor, are you OK? Should we call for help?"

Pastor Davis coughed a few times and then drew in a raspy breath. "I… I… think… well, my nerves aren't what they used to be. When people act in an aggressive way toward me… Well, I'm sorry for my reaction. I think I need to go lie down now if you don't mind. Please excuse me. Dear? Are you coming with me?"

"I'll just show these young men out, honey. You go on and lie down. It's time for your afternoon nap anyway." Mrs Davis turned her stern features on the two detectives. "Sit back down. Let's have a talk."

***

The detectives were heading back to the station with more questions than answers. The money provided by the generous donor performed a function above keeping the doors open; it provided for all the utilities, building maintenance and a generous salary for the pastor. The church also had a benevolence fund that made them the target for a lot of inner-city ne'er-do-wells looking for a handout.

Was the benefactor truly that altruistic or did he have something to gain from the arrangement? What had he been using the church for? It was evident he had prepared a meal that demonstrated the abilities of a professional chef. Perhaps that would be a good place to begin the search.

Chapter Twenty

"Turn right here!" Mama shouted.

Anna stepped on the brake and was barely able to make the turn without running into the other car sitting at the intersection. All she saw of the driver was an open mouth and owl eyes. Now that driver would probably remember this van that almost wiped her out. They needed to be more careful.

"Mama, you've led me down one street after another for the past forty-five minutes. Do you remember where your doctor friend is or not?"

"I do remember. Sort of. His nephew put him in a nursing home too. All he did was have a few falls at his house and there he was — put out to pasture like an old horse. An old, useless horse! Hmmmpf!"

"Oh my!" Anna sighed. "OK, Mama. A nursing home? Seriously? Mama, how is this man going to help us?"

"Just because he's old doesn't mean he isn't skilled. He can be trusted too. If we can just find him. Hmmmmm. I've been here before. It looks kinda familiar... I just can't... Where are we going again?

Anna wanted to bang her head into something. The frustration… From the back seat, she heard Edith. "Anna, I'm checking Google for nursing homes around our current location. There's one hidden at the back of a subdivision. Turn left up here."

Now there were two elderly ladies giving her directions. "Mama, do you even know if your friend is still alive? How old is he?"

"Oh, he's only about ten years older than me. I'm sure he's alive. I would have been notified if he had died. I'm listed as a medical contact."

"Mama, he's eight years old now." Anna was thinking that her mother might have been told that her friend had passed away but just didn't remember it. Mama tended to forget unpleasant things more than pleasant, which was probably a good way to be — up to a point.

EVANGELINE SKILLED NURSING SERVICE. The sign was small, but Anna was looking for it. The arrow directed her down a narrow, tree-lined drive that ended in a full parking lot in front of a red-brick building. Azaleas and crape myrtles dotted the tastefully done landscape. It looked like a resort. Maybe this would be a good place to move Mama, once they made sure she was safe. Hopefully her doctor friend was alive.

Mama was practically jumping up and down in her excitement to see her old friend.

Edith was more difficult to get out of the van than Mama was. Finally, Anna gave up and asked if she would rather just stay put and rest some more. It was nearly spring so the weather hadn't turned hot yet, and they were parked under a shady live oak tree. "I'll put down all the windows. Edith, just lie there and rest. Mama and I will go for help."

Anna wheeled Mama into the home. They went straight down the main hall and stopped in front of the nurse's desk where Mama took over. "I'm here to see my friend Doctor Phillip Karns. I'm on his list. I'd like to check him out."

"Oh! Let me just see here. Oh yes. I see your name, Elizabeth Satterfield," said the nurse. "Let me go see if he's up for an outing."

"Elizabeth Satterfield?" asked Anna.

"Nice name, isn't it?"

"Is it yours?"

"Ha! What do you think?"

Another lie! Anna looked down the hall as the nurse wheeled a beaming man in a brown corduroy jacket toward them. Even if Anna hadn't known the man was a retired doctor, that's just what she would have pegged him for. He wore round spectacles and his feet on the rests of the wheelchair were clad in a pair of Bass Weejuns that looked like they were from the 1960s. He gave the appearance of someone who would take care of himself and everyone around him with immaculate precision. For some reason, Anna felt like she'd known him her whole life.

"Oh, Phil! Phil!" Mama sang out. They reached their arms out to each other and clasped hands as their chairs got near enough.

"I hear we're going out. Are you our chaperone, Anna?" the doctor asked.

"You know my name?"

"Oh, my dear girl. I know far more than your name. I can't say how happy I am to see you."

Anna wondered — another puzzle?

Chapter Twenty-One

It felt like he was on a comfortable bed, which was not what he was expecting, as he regained consciousness. "OK, Pierre, we know you're awake."

"My name is Pierce."

"What kind of a name is Pierce? I think I'll call you Pierre, a good French-Canadian name, or maybe you prefer Louisiana Cajun French?" the unseen voice taunted. The bag had been removed, but Pierce dreaded opening his eyes. As long as his eyes were closed, he could deny the reality that he had been sloppy enough to get picked up off the street.

"What do you want?" Pierce groaned, still feeling headachy and sick after whatever was in the syringe that they had plunged into him.

"Oh, come now, Pierre. Let's not play games; we're both professionals."

"Look, we're part of the same organization." Pierce hoped the man could be reasoned with. After all, he was a Canadian who was polite enough to tie him to a comfortable bed rather than a steel chair in a leaky basement.

"That might have worked had the mark not killed my man. That man was my friend. I don't forget a thing like that. The money... pfhht... that would be nothing. I can pick up another mark by tomorrow morning, but friends aren't that easy to come by."

"I'm sorry about your friend. I'm sure it was an accident. You do know that two of the women who entered that church are over seventy and the other one has no training whatsoever. I don't know how they could have overpowered a trained assassin."

"Overpower him? No. Outsmart him? Quite possibly. My friend had many skills, murder, torture, intimidation, but thinking — that was not really one of them. Still, I loved him like a brother. Actually, he was more than a friend. He was my cousin."

"What do you hope to gain by keeping me? I can't tell you anything you don't already know."

"I have no need for your information. You are just, shall we say, a piece of cheese for my little mousetrap."

"What makes you think they're even looking for me?"

"Oh, Pierre, do not take me for a fool! Even though our units are separate, and wisely so, that does not mean that I don't know your history. Pierre — son of Trident! Yes, you will be missed... and then sought. I'll have the cook bring you a sandwich. I hope it will be acceptable to your most discerning palate."

Pierce's wrists were in handcuffs with a chain connected to the ankle cuffs, which then fastened around the leg of the antique iron bed. He scanned the situation, beginning with how the bed was constructed. It was a beautiful, high fluffy bed that fitted in well with the room, lofty ceilings, tall windows, antebellum style wallpaper. He managed to sit up and peer out the window. He could see the huge, moss-covered live oaks, magnolias and crape myrtles dotting the sweeping lawn with the bayou flowing where the property line apparently ended. At least it looked like he was still in Louisiana. There were very few places that had that particular, distinctive aspect of architecture and landscape. He felt mildly comforted by the thought.

The door squeaked as it slowly swung into the room. A young Creole fellow peered around the side of the six-panel door. As he balanced a tray in one hand, he put his other hand with a finger to his lips to shush Pierce. Pierce knew enough not to let on that the young man was familiar, but his heart skipped a beat with joy.

Trais set the sandwich and drink on a table next to the bed. When Pierce opened his mouth to whisper, Trais shook his head 'no'. Pierce got the message. Then his friend quietly closed the door behind him as he went out.

Chapter Twenty-Two

Detectives Brown and MacGregor circled around The Rice Bowl restaurant checking it out. First, they noted and photographed the signs on the front and back doors. Then they walked around peeking in windows. It had been three days since the apparent shooting at the church. Financial records had brought them to the owner of this establishment, Pierce Andrews. He had a spotless record, but something here was fishier than his famous stuffed red fish on a bed of wild rice.

They pulled out a map of the city, spread it across the rear of their patrol car, and looked at the places they had marked — the restaurant, the church, and one other location. They had found Pierce's beige Camry, so they knew he didn't drive away in it. He would probably have to walk to where he could hunker down without being noticed. In the five-mile radius they had drawn around the church, there were various inexpensive motels. When checked out, none of them showed any sign of the missing man.

Detective MacGregor looked off into the distance as he tapped the third small circle on the map — Good

Shepherd Homeless Shelter. "Let's go," he told his partner. "One more place to check."

Police detectives in nondescript suits brandishing badges were not a terribly uncommon sight at the shelter. Todd gave his best, welcoming smile as he received the stern pair into the front room of his establishment. "What can I do to serve the city today?" he asked.

The police showed him the enlarged picture taken from Pierce's driver's license.

"Oh dear. I wondered why he disappeared so suddenly. Has he done something wrong? I hope not. He seemed such a nice man, great cook too. He's not hurt or… anything… is he?"

"He should have been a great cook. He's a world-renowned chef — the owner of The Rice Bowl. Ever heard of it?" questioned Brown.

"Sure! Who hasn't? Never been able to afford to go. Whoo-eee, who would have guessed that he made breakfast for our guys. Sure wish I had been here that morning to have tasted it. I heard it was a miracle of Spam and Velveeta. I wonder if he'll put that on his menu now. Ha!" Todd was obviously quite amused with himself, but he sobered up quickly when he grasped that the detectives weren't enjoying his humor.

"Do you know what happened to him?" Detective MacGregor asked.

"Wish I did! He kinda stood us up for dinner. The guys were pretty disappointed when they came in and saw it was me in the kitchen instead of him."

"So, he just disappeared?"

"Totally! All his stuff was still in his room. We put it in the locker over there if you want to take a look at it." Todd walked over to the lockers, unlocked one, and pulled the small duffle bag out. "Here. All yours! Can you let me know what happened? Is he OK? Why are you looking for him?

"Sorry. Police business," Brown said. "Give us every detail about him from the moment he walked in your door to the last second you saw him."

"I can only tell you about what I know. Any other details you need to get from the day guy, Michael. I do know that Joe, he told us his name is Joe, needed to find a new job. He said he was going to check databases and papers and stuff at the library. It's in walking distance, so he headed out the door toward the library the last we saw him around here. Talk to Michael. He's the one who told me."

"Thanks. We'll do that."

"Do you need his address?"

"No. We got it."

"Oh! How silly of me. Of course you…"

They were out of the door before Todd finished his sarcasm. He didn't know what all that was about, but he was sure that Joe or Pierce or whatever he needed to call himself wasn't a criminal. He felt like he had been around enough to spot one when he saw one, and Pierce wasn't that. He wasn't sure what he was, but certainly not a criminal. If he came across him again, Todd decided that he'd give him any help he could.

Chapter Twenty-Three

Anna was glad she had her bank cards because this endeavor was likely going to cost. If one must be faced with danger and disaster, it's easier having access to a few funds. Her properties in Indiana had made her bank account comfortably fat while she had been working on getting her business going in Louisiana. She had her eye on several possibilities, and her realtor was busy negotiating a promising one north of Lake Pontchartrain.

That area had experienced a boom since Hurricane Katrina had sent many New Orleans residents, at least those who weren't in love with the city, looking for higher ground. There were still lots of opportunities there, and Anna had decided she'd take part in them.

She didn't have a qualm as she handed the card to the receptionist. "I have adjoining rooms for you, as requested," the young man said with his bright smile and chipper voice. Anna was too tired for chipper right now. She exited the lobby and pulled the van to the back of the building where they could enter their rooms facing the parking lot. It wasn't glamorous, but it was adequate. It had the added bonuses of being slightly out of the way and appearing clean. Clean was important right now.

After pushing Mama's and the doctor's chairs into the room, Anna went back for Edith.

"Anna's a big wuss when it comes to blood. I don't want her in the room with me while you fix me up. The last thing I need is to see her white face as she hits the floor in her dainty faint." Edith managed to say all this as she leaned on Anna and struggled into her room.

"Thanks for all the support and appreciation, Aunt Edith."

"How many times do I have to tell you...- Oh never mind. I really do appreciate you, dear, but am I lying?" Edith waited for Anna to answer, but there was only silence. "OK. Thought not. Well, get on over to your safe place and let the grownups deal with me."

Without a word, Anna opened the adjoining door and stumbled to the bed in exhaustion. She fell over like a felled tree, and the word 'timber' was her last conscious thought as she hit the sheets.

Even in her fatigue, she couldn't stop her dreams. "Where's Mama?" she was screaming at her dream daddy. "Why don't you care? Why do you let her treat you the way she does?" Anna remembered, in her dream, the safe feeling that Daddy would always be there and would always look after her. As she grew older, she had the dreaded fear that her mother's bad behavior would drive away the only stabilizing force in her life. She knew that he had his strong group of supportive male friends. She knew he would never cheat on Mama the way Anna was sure Mama had done to him.

Then, while she was in her sophomore year in college, Daddy got that horrible wasting disease that killed him with ruthless speed. Anna's dream changed to the graveside. Mama hadn't bothered to attend. There were just Daddy's friends… and they sobbed like children. Anna stood between her brother and sister. Her strongest emotion was simply — emptiness.

Chapter Twenty-Four

Trais walked back from the dock where he had purchased a nice bag of shrimp directly from the boat as it came in after several exhausting days on the ocean. Gulf shrimp were a real treat and his employers couldn't get enough of them. That was one reason they hired Trais. He promised them an excellent deal on their favorite food and a wide repertoire of recipes to make their taste buds dance for joy. The owner of the boat greeted Trais with restraint, as usual.

Trais' family had been in the shrimping business for three generations. His two older brothers still worked with their dad, who had a hard time reconciling with the fact that his third son, thus the name Trais, had chosen to become a chef instead. Trais had been trained by a master — Pierce. Taking this small, private job was beneath his skill level, but he had his reasons.

He walked into the back door of the mansion and headed for the kitchen. He was greeted by the obvious leader of the pair, Liam. "Hi, Trais! You got us some more fresh shrimps, aye?"

"Yep, straight off the boat."

"I'm so glad we hired someone with connections — food connections that is. You know, espionage runs on its stomach. Ha, ha, ha, ha!"

Trais did his best to join in the laughter, but he found everything Liam said to be a little twisted, in spite of his polite Canadian reputation.

"I'll just get to work cleaning and deveining these shrimps in time for dinner."

"OK. Don't let me stand in your way. I'm sure our guest upstairs will be ready for a good meal after having nothing but a sandwich all day. Hey, did you know he's a famous chef?"

"You don't say?" said Trais ducking his head to hide his smirk. "Well, I hope I don't shame myself too much with my cooking."

"I think you do quite well for an amateur, Trais."

Trais felt a bit chagrined, but didn't show it, in the humiliating effort to maintain his cover. He had seen no reason not to give his real name. He hadn't distinguished himself with The Cooking School organization well enough yet to be known by anyone but his mentor, Pierce.

He had practically begged Pierce for the job when he was sixteen so he could get off the streets and have regular meals. He couldn't handle the pressure his dad put on him so, as a rebellious teenager, he ran away from home. Pierce had seen something in him that he felt he could cultivate. Not only Trais' love of cooking, but his shrewd street-smarts made for great potential in the off-the-books network of government trained assassins.

They never killed anyone who wasn't an imminent threat to the safety and security of ordinary, freedom loving folks. Trais had seen people die on the streets all the time for no reason at all except pride or territory. But Pierce wasn't a killer; he was an organizer, and Trais needed a solid, dependable person in his life to give him guidance in the profession he had chosen for himself. He couldn't imagine living out his life on a grueling shrimp boat. He looked up to Pierce. He was like the father Trais had wished his own had been. No one was going to hurt him or anyone who mattered to him, at least not while Trais was around.

Trais was looking for a way to impart to Pierce that he was keeping his eyes and ears open to step in and turn the tide of events at the proper moment, but Liam wasn't allowing anyone else to speak to Pierce. Liam delivered Pierce's dinner that night. Pierce recognized his own recipe for shrimp creole. The seasonings were perfect. He felt pride for his protégé.

"How do you intend to use me as bait to lure your mark in here? You don't know where they are, do you?" Pierce asked Liam.

"Now, that's not your concern, is it? Looks like you're enjoying the food. That young fella must be a pretty good cook for someone like you to appreciate it so much," Liam observed.

"I always like sampling other people's dishes. You might be surprised, but I can get tired of the taste of my own cooking. It's a pleasure to try someone else's, especially someone who knows how to do justice to a good, fresh shrimp."

"I guess whipping up delicacies must come naturally to you Louisiana people."

"Yeah. I'm sure that's it. But you're part of The Cooking School. Don't you cook?"

"You don't have to know how to cook to post recipes with hidden messages online. You just chose to get more involved in that part, and it's been a good cover for you. I have my own particular cover."

"What might that be? if you don't mind my asking," Pierce questioned.

"I don't mind your asking if you don't mind my not telling. I expect you to come out of this situation alive. I have no intention of taking out your effective unit. When all this is over, I don't want you knowing where I am, get what I mean?" Liam raised his eyebrow at Pierce.

"OK. Whatever. Now, can you just let me enjoy the rest of my meal in peace?" Pierce didn't like being in the dark like this, especially when people needed him. The feeling of powerlessness weighed on his heart.

Chapter Twenty-Five

After Edith's wound was cleaned and stitched, Dr Karns sat there admiring his work. "That was very satisfying. It's been a long time. Thank you for the opportunity, Trident."

"Don't mention it," Edith groused. "I mean it. Really. Please don't mention it again. It was hard waiting so long for medical treatment, and for you to enjoy it this much is just… unsettling, to put it mildly."

"Well, look at it from my perspective. I've been tucked away, out of use, out of the loop, out of everything I've ever held dear, and for you to come along and bring all these things back to me, I just can't thank you enough. Sorry you had to suffer a bit in the process."

"Yes, well, it has been quite an ordeal for this old gal. We're all just completely exhausted at this point. I'll order us a pizza and we should just use the rest of this day and tonight to relax before we make any further decisions. I think Anna's down for the count. I'll call the order in. What do you both want?"

When they finished eating, they put the rest of the pizza into the mini fridge, so Anna could heat it in the room microwave when she woke up. No one wanted to disturb her.

"I'll sleep in the second bed in this room with Anna. You two can have this room. We'll leave the connecting door open in case y'all need anything."

"Why should we need anything?" Dr Karns asked. Pelican was in one of her passive moods and hadn't said anything for some time.

"Well, you're both in wheelchairs."

"The only reason I'm in this chair is to 'keep me from falling'. I haven't fallen in ages."

Probably because you've been in a wheelchair and watched carefully, Edith thought, but knew better than to say this out loud. "So, you think you need that much privacy? I would really feel better if we leave the door open. The lights will be off and I don't know exactly how safe we are here. We should be OK, but better safe than sorry."

"So we're arguing in clichés now?"

"Whatever. I'm too tired for games. Goodnight."

Pelican apparently got into one of her talking moods once the lights were out. She and the doctor whispered and giggled far into the night. *More power to them! Another cliché,* Edith thought as she drifted into a dreamless sleep.

At least she thought it was dreamless. Was she dreaming now as she heard scraping sounds in the doorknob and then the door hinges squeaking slightly? She was suddenly alert and reaching for the gun under her pillow. She saw two shadows creeping across the room silhouetted by the nightlight. She used her deepest, most menacing voice. "I'm armed and a crack shot. I will not hesitate to end your life this instant unless you stop and identify yourselves."

The man in the lead let out a huff and said, "All right, so you got me. What now?"

"Identify yourself."

"If I do that, you won't know if I'm telling the truth."

"Right now, I recognize your voice." Edith felt the tension drain from her. "Little Manny? Is that you?"

Emmanuel told his companion by the door to flip on the light. As everyone was squinting and adjusting to the sudden brightness, he said, "Aunt Edith! Is that you?"

"Oh! My goodness! Little Manny! It's been forever! Look at you all grown up… and stealing into old ladies' bedrooms in the dead of night. Emmanuel Senior should tan your hide!"

"Aunt Edith! What are you doing here? My unit was told to silence a mark that knew too much and was threatening The Cooking School and the safety of our respective nations."

"Is that all you know about your mark, Manny?"

"We were given demographic details and a picture."

"Let me see that picture." Edith picked up her glasses from the bedside table and examined the picture. "This was taken twenty years ago. She posed in this picture with the intention of looking intimidating, but if you saw her now… Oh, Manny, Manny. Why is everyone so quick to take someone out without understanding why?"

"We've never been told details except what was strictly need-to-know."

"It's evident to me that our organization is changing, and not for the better, much like our politicians. We were once so idealistic, so patriotic… but now…" Edith looked so sad that Manny sat down next to her and put his arm around her to comfort her.

"What can I do to make you better, Aunt Edith?"

"You see the young woman in the bed next to mine pretending to be asleep?" At this, Anna opened her eyes and sat up with a cat just swallowed the canary expression.

Manny stuck out his hand and Anna gave it a perfunctory shake. "Allow me to introduce myself," he said. "My name is Emmanuel Stefanos Junior. This sweet lady beside me is my aunt."

"Is she now?" asked Anna with no attempt to mask her sarcasm.

"Yes. My father is married to her sister. We don't use her real name outside of our house. We call her Edith."

"I always thought her sister was my mother."

Manny's eyebrows shot up and he gave his aunt a quizzical look.

"Long story," she said.

"Would you all please be quiet? My sweetie and I are trying to sleep!" came the quavering male voice from the next room.

"Your sweetie? How many secrets do all of you have? My head is spinning!" Anna put her hands to the sides of her head.

Manny looked at Edith, "What's with her? She's sure got her panties in a wad."

"Please, Manny. Try to avoid clichés. I've had enough of them for a while.

Manny looked even more puzzled. "Whatever you want." He stopped himself just before he said, *Your wish is my command.*

Chapter Twenty-Six

"Why don't we split up today? You interview everyone you can at that homeless shelter, and I'll track down everyone I can at the restaurant. It's still shut down so the workers are probably getting a little antsy and ready to talk," Detective MacGregor said.

"Sounds good to me. We'll meet back here later and compare notes," Brown agreed.

***

After interviewing the sous chef and several servers, MacGregor had come up with a name, Trais Fuqua. He found out that his dad owned a shrimp boat down the bayou in the backwater town of Cocodrie. It would take a couple of hours to get there so he hoped he wasn't wasting his day.

The drive was long and boring after passing through the town of Houma. There was nothing but swamps and cypress trees to add to the monotony. Every now and then, there would be a rickety trailer home with old tires piled on the roof. He found his mind wandering about why someone would do that as he pulled into the unincorporated fishing town.

After walking around, he was pointed in the direction of the shrimp boat he was hunting for. He watched as a young man was handed a large bag of shrimp and then jumped on a bicycle, securing his haul in a basket on the back. Then the middle-aged fisherman hung his head and turned back onto his boat.

"Excuse me!" MacGregor called. "Are you Mr Fuqua?"

The expression on the weathered brown face didn't change as he recognized the type of the man who was asking. He didn't need to see the badge. "What can I do for you?"

"I'm looking for your son, Trais."

"Well, you just missed him. He's on a bike, so if you're driving, you can catch him. I can't imagine what you'd need him for. He's been working hard and staying out of trouble, as much as I can tell."

"Yes. Right. Well, he's not in trouble, but he might have some information I'm in need of."

"I don't think I can help you there." Fuqua turned back onto his boat.

"I'm sorry to bother you, but if I can just have a minute of your time," MacGregor pressed.

Fuqua reluctantly turned a mournful face toward the detective and waited silently for an explanation.

"Do you know if your son knows the owner of a restaurant called The Rice Bowl?"

"Could be. My son wants to be a chef. Though I could sure use him here. I guess he's just too soft for my kind of business. A bit of a letdown to be honest."

"Is there anything more you can tell me?"

"I don't know what he's doing right now, but he seems pretty sneaky about it. It worries me a bit. Way off down here in Cocodrie. I mean, we have some restaurants hereabouts, little hole-in-the-wall shacks, but nothing like out there in New Orleans where he run off to."

"How often do you see him, Mr Fuqua?"

"I went months without seeing him. Now I see him nearly every day. I don't know what made the change. I got a good haul of shrimp iced down in the hold. He'll probably be back for some more tomorrow. Then, I have to head back out to sea for a couple of days to bring in some more. They got to be fresh or folks will quit doing business. Keeps me pretty wore out."

"Mr Fuqua, would you have any other appropriate clothing for me to borrow to blend in on your boat so I can have a chance for a little chat with your son tomorrow?"

Mr Fuqua frowned and hedged about the strange request. "I won't allow anything to hurt my son. He's disappointed me, but he's still family. No one messes with my family."

"I'm afraid that may be what we're dealing with here, sir. I'm afraid your son may be under the influence of some very dangerous characters. I don't know many details now. That's why I need to talk with him, to make sure he's safe."

As hardened by back-breaking work as Fuqua was, he still had a soft spot for his youngest son. "Me and my boys will do whatever needs to be done to help you look after Trais."

"Thank you, sir. I'll see you tomorrow morning."

"Oh, about those clothes. Just worn-out jeans, a ragged shirt, and run-down work boots should do you. Goodwill would be my suggestion."

"See you tomorrow." MacGregor waved as he turned back toward his car.

Chapter Twenty-Seven

From the adjoining room, they heard Mama screaming. Anna threw back the covers and ran to her mother. She was on the floor next to the bed. The bathroom light was thankfully left on so Anna didn't step on her.

"Mama! Mama! What happened?"

Her mother was mumbling incoherently and shaking all over. "Ma... ma... man! Strange man!"

"Mama, that's your old friend, Doctor Karns!" Anna informed her.

"Who?" Mama questioned, looking confused.

"Mama, how did you get on the floor?" Anna reached behind Mama's shoulders and helped her to sit up.

"I don't know." Mama looked around the dimly lit room. "Where are we?" She reached out and clutched Anna's hand in fear.

The simple act brought a lump to Anna's throat. It was hard to see her strong, decisive mother brought to such weakness and confusion.

"Can someone please help me get my mother up?" Anna called to the group standing in the doorway staring uncertainly into the room.

The men sprang into action and quickly picked Mama up and sat her on the side of the bed.

"There's still a strange man in my bed," Mama whined piteously.

"Sweetie, it's me, Phil," the doctor explained.

"You're not Phil!" Mama was nearly shouting in her increased agitation. "You look nothing like my Phil! You're old! Get away from me!"

Doctor Karns struggled to get out of the bed. Manny went around and helped him. "Young man, I hate to ask, but could you assist me to the restroom?"

Manny settled him into his chair and dutifully took him to the restroom. Once he had left the room, Mama was able to calm down slightly, but she still acted frightened and confused. Anna talked with her softly and gently until light began to dawn in Mama's eyes.

"Oh! Yes. OK. I remember now."

Anna wasn't completely sure if Mama really remembered or if she just wanted them to think she did. Although she was losing her memory and her reasoning skills, she was still pretty crafty at trying to cover her difficulties. It made Anna perpetually feel like she was off-balance. She was learning about Alzheimer's as she went along, and every time she felt like she understood, more changes occurred.

Anna looked at Mama, then at Edith, and then down at herself. They all looked wrinkled and ragged. If they were going to go out into the public, something would need to be done about their clothing situation. Probably a trip to Goodwill would be the best plan. They wouldn't stand out as badly walking in there. First, they would have to get their whole group back to New Orleans.

Manny and his unnamed friend — he said to call him John — decided to follow the van to the epicenter of their situation. They no longer felt like they should eliminate this target, but they were trying to form plans to look after her. They agreed that it wasn't right to take out an old lady who had been a valued asset for so many years just because she had lost her reasoning and discretion. But they also knew that something would have to be done to protect their organization from exposure. After both vehicles exited the drive-through at McDonalds, they headed south.

Chapter Twenty-Eight

They pulled into the parking lot at the big Goodwill store in Metairie. Anna pushed Mama's chair as Edith took control of the doctor's. People held open the store doors and looked with sympathy at the poor, rumpled group.

Anna quickly thumbed through men's shirts while the doctor looked on and stated either approval or disapproval for her selections. Everyone figured they should get two changes of clothes since they didn't know how long this difficulty would last. Doctor Karns' chair was blocking the aisle as an impatient man was trying to find some clothes for himself. When he made his way around him, all the man seemed interested in were the most ragged, unattractive shirts. Anna had always been curious and outgoing, so she couldn't help herself from asking the man if he was looking for costumes for the stage.

"Something like that," the man mumbled.

"Something like that? What's like the stage? Oh! Is it like some kind of undercover work? You do kinda look like a policeman."

The man looked quizzically at Anna. "You ask a lot of questions."

"Sorry. I'm just a very curious person. It's been a curse since childhood." She stuck out her hand. "My name's Anna."

Detective MacGregor chose to use a fake name and the first one that came to mind was… "Glad to meet you. Name's Pierce."

Anna just looked at him with her mouth hanging open. *No! It's been a long time, but this guy's too old to be him! There's more than one Pierce in this city, I'm sure,* she thought.

When she didn't speak, MacGregor picked up his shirt and walked away shaking his head. "This city sure is full of strange people," he muttered to himself.

After a complicated procedure to get everyone's clothes changed in the store's restroom, they packed the rest of their belongings into a large duffle bag they had bought at the second-hand store, and headed to a Walmart for essentials like toothbrushes and extra underwear.

This was becoming a very long day for the elderly folks, and it was obviously wearing them down. Anna found them a hotel that would suit their needs and ordered Chinese takeout. Their Haitian friends got a room down the hall.

Before the order arrived, she excused herself and said she'd be back soon. Her exhausted traveling companions barely registered her exit. Back in the van, she brought up The Rice Bowl on her phone's GPS. They were going to have to find Pierce and this was the only lead they currently had. She started up the old vehicle with a rumble and pulled out onto the cracked asphalt.

The GPS didn't let her down, and parking at the restaurant, she checked out her surroundings. Sliding from the hot, vinyl driver's seat, she walked carefully up to the back door. The sign Pierce had made was still hanging there. She took out a pen and wrote, *Sorry we keep missing each other. Please give me a call at* — here she added a phone number — *Love, Mom.* That should do it, she figured, as she walked back to the van.

Chapter Twenty-Nine

Liam's plan was to leave a note on the restaurant. It was the only place of contact he knew for Pierce's mom, who he knew was helping his mark. He got ready to pull into the parking lot when he noticed the slender lady walking toward the large conversion van. He watched her climb into the cumbersome vehicle and pull away. He then pulled in, parked and ambled carefully toward the back door, observing everything from the corner of his eye.

The note Pierce had left was still there, but written at the bottom of it in blue ink was what he was hoping to find. He ripped the whole note off the door and shoved it into his pocket with a smile. Things were finally coming together. He would get his payment and his revenge.

***

The next morning, Trais rode his bicycle down to the pier to buy some shrimp and oysters for the day's cuisine. He knew everyone who worked around there, so he was surprised to see a new face come off the boat to greet him instead of his father. The man's clothes bespoke the rough life, but his grooming said otherwise. Trais approached him carefully. "Where's my dad, and who are you?"

"Trais, my name is Detective MacGregor. I don't know what you've gotten mixed up in, but I'm here to help you."

"You don't know what you're getting mixed up in!" Trais mimicked. "You need to clear out of here quick before anyone sees you. Lives are at stake and you're messing with my operation."

"Your operation?" MacGregor raised his eyebrows in surprise. "Who are you with?"

"That's not your business. Just give me my shrimp and leave!"

"Trais, I know that your friend is missing and could be in grave danger. If you're in this on your own, I'd like for you to consider me an ally. Let me help you."

Trais thought for a minute. "I probably could use some help, but you can't tell anyone else on the force. It has to be just you."

"Count on it. I won't tell anyone unless circumstances make it necessary."

"OK. Mess up your hair. Put on an old hat, and please, get your hands and face dirty, especially those fingernails."

MacGregor looked down at his clean hands and evenly trimmed nails. He had a point. From a distance, he could fool someone, but certainly not up close. "I'll take care of this right away. In the meantime, we need to make some plans. I'm assuming someone is holding Pierce hostage. Can you tell me why?"

"That's got to be part of our deal. I belong to an organization of patriots that you cannot know about or ask about. Got that?"

"I don't like it, but I'm willing to go along... for now."

"Now is all we have, isn't it? I can't stay long without causing suspicion so let's make this fast." Trais walked into the ship's cabin with the detective. There was no sign of his dad, which made Trais feel a little better as he quickly discussed a plan to save lives and free his friend.

Chapter Thirty

$\mathcal{E}$dith's training never left her, even when she wasn't using it on a regular basis, so the slight shuffling noise was enough to bring her wide awake. She cracked her eyes open but made sure not to change the cadence of her breathing to cause anyone nearby to notice her. Across the room, Anna was sitting in a chair with the lamp pointed down on a book in her hands. Edith could tell she was trying to be quiet in order not to disturb her roommate.

Edith took a deep breath in relief. "Anna, what are you doing? What time is it?"

"It's about six-thirty, Aunt Edith. I'm sorry if I woke you."

"I told you I'm not your aunt."

"Yes. I know, and I've been thinking about it. You've been my aunt my whole life. I love you like my aunt and I don't intend to change my feelings for you. I don't want to make you angry or anything, but I would appreciate it if you would honor me by continuing to be my aunt."

Edith felt the unexpected lump rising in her throat. "Ahem." She cleared her throat and spoke more abruptly than she intended. "OK. Whatever makes you happy."

Then she smiled to soften the harshness she hadn't intended to impart.

Anna returned the smile and then redirected her attention back to the book in her lap.

"What is it you're reading there, girl… Anna?" Edith inquired, trying to make amends.

"I read every morning when I'm not running for my life. I'm glad this hotel put one into the room. I've been missing my morning devotion."

"What? Is that a Bible? Really? I didn't know anyone read one of those . It's pretty outdated, isn't it?" Edith was trying not to sound like she was making light of how Anna chose to start her morning, but it was hard to keep the mild derision out of her voice.

"Aunt Edith, how did you get here?" Anna asked.

"Um, in a van?" Edith knew she was being somewhat silly, but she considered the whole concept silly.

"You know what I mean. I know a lot of people think we're all an accident, but think about it. What's the point if we don't have a creator who has a plan for everything?"

"What's the point? Well, survival, I guess."

"For what purpose?"

"Well, to propagate the species, I guess."

"What would be the purpose of that if we are just born and then die and cease to exist? What's the point of anything if that's all there is?"

"But there was a big bang, then dust, then light, then water, then amoeba, then fish, birds, large animals and people."

"But… dust? Where did the dust come from?"

"Well, that's the mystery, isn't it?"

"Actually, it isn't a mystery. The most logical explanation is that there is a God who created everything for his own pleasure. He made man to worship and love Him. He planned everything out of His great wisdom, even a way for us to have an intimate relationship with Him. He walked on this Earth He made, gave His life for His puny creatures, and planned an eternity for those who love Him to enjoy together. He worked it all out from before the ages began.

"That's why I read the Bible. It is His letter to us. It guides and comforts. That's why I'm not worried about the outcome of all this. The whole thing blindsided me and sent me into rather a tailspin, but I've gotten my heart settled by reading His Word to me. He has it under control. Would you like to pray with me, Aunt Edith?"

"No one has ever asked me to pray with them," Edith said in wonder. "I don't even know what it would be like. It seems a little unnerving."

Anna walked across the room and sat down on the edge of Edith's bed. She took her hand and bowed her head. When she finished, Edith took a quivering breath and gave Anna a genuine hug. "I don't know why, but I do feel better. Thank you. That was… well… um… new, different, but I liked it. But Anna, you don't know the things I've done in my life!".

"God knows, Aunt Edith. Nothing is hidden from Him. He sent His son, who is God, to die to take away your sins."

"I've heard that somewhere before but it makes no sense. How can someone else take away my sins?"

"Think of it like you're badly in debt and someone comes along and pays all your bills."

"That would make anyone happy. So, why doesn't everyone know about this?" Edith asked in surprise.

"The information is available to them, but it takes more than information to believe. God gives faith as a gift. A gift isn't something you demand or manipulate; it is just given. Do you have faith, Aunt Edith?"

"You know, it's strange, but I think I do!" Edith said.

"You already said you've done a lot of bad things. The truth is, everyone has. Acknowledge that, believe that his sacrificial death on the cross was for your forgiveness, and you will be His. He takes care of His own. Even in bad things, He brings about His good. You'll never be alone again, Aunt Edith."

"I feel so… light… so new! I never knew this was even possible. Why didn't I know?" Edith questioned incredulously.

"Remember I said God had everything planned out in advance?"

"Yes."

"He even had this moment set aside. This very moment, this very gift. Isn't it wonderful?" Anna asked with a smile.

Tears were running down Edith's face. "You truly are my family, Anna. I love you! Now, let's go find the will of God and do as He directs. We've got some loved ones to help!"

Chapter Thirty-One

Trais was busy cleaning up after another successful meal. Cooking delicious food gave him a deep sense of satisfaction that he didn't get from many other pursuits. His dad would never understand this.

He paused in his work and perceived that something didn't feel right. It was too quiet. He threw the dishtowel over his shoulder and went out of the kitchen, through the dining room, and into the living room. Usually, one or both of the men were watching TV. He saw through the window to where the car was supposed to be parked. It was gone.

Trais walked out onto the porch and looked down the road. There was no trace of his employers. He went back in and quickly scaled the sweeping staircase to the stately second floor. When he peered down the hallway, he noticed that the door to the room where Pierce was kept locked away was standing open. *Oh no!* He crept slowly toward the room, dreading what he knew he'd find. Pierce's bed was empty. He was gone, along with the handcuffs and chains that had kept him bound to his bed. Trais felt a sick feeling in the pit of his stomach. He had failed his friend.

After receiving the phone call, Anna told Edith that it was time to go make the exchange for Pierce. "We are not giving Pelican to those murderers!" Edith stormed.

"I know we can't do that, but we have to at least try to convince them that they don't want to kill her."

Edith exclaimed, "I have an idea! They're looking for an elderly lady. They have an old picture of your mother. If I wrap up in shawls and get into her wheelchair, I can possibly fool strangers into thinking I'm Pelican. Where is the exchange to be made?"

"I have an address on Bourbon Street," Anna answered with a face showing her distaste.

"Why would they want to do it there?"

"I guess that will make us easy to spot. Not many elderly ladies hang out in that neighborhood. But I think it's to our advantage. Lots of people around."

"Drunks and people who think everything's a show. Let's get ready."

"Lock and load," Anna said.

"Lock and load?" Edith whispered. "I've created a monster!" She couldn't help but laugh to herself. "Anna, could we pray first?"

***

Bourbon Street was just the way Anna remembered it from when she had come down as a teenager with her friends. At that time, all she cared about was impressing her small group. Now, she noticed the large billboards with various advertisements for the entertainments available.

She nearly ran the wheelchair into a sidewalk advertising placard showing a nude woman who must have weighed over five hundred pounds. Her most private parts were obscured by the skirt of fat skin hanging down in front of her. She had a salacious grin on her face. Anna couldn't figure out the appeal.

She watched overhead and saw a swing coming in and out of an upstairs window with a topless woman sitting on the seat. She had to look again before it became apparent that the woman was a mannequin.

There was a different type of street musician on each corner. Some were quite good. There were three young boys playing Zydeco music. They appeared to be brothers ranging in age from probably about ten to the oldest one who looked about eighteen. The accordion the smallest boy was playing looked way too heavy for him. Anna had learned long ago not to be impressed with this skill. All the Zydeco songs sounded almost exactly alike. If you learned to play one song, you could play them all.

People staggered down the road; many seemed way too drunk for it to only be about nine o'clock. They had undoubtedly been drinking all day. Anna steered the wheelchair around the feet of someone sleeping with his head in an enclave and the rest of him partially blocking the sidewalk. She noticed the large wet spot on the front of his pants. She shuddered at the sight.

The police would be along soon to pick him up and let him sleep it off somewhere away from the tourists that filled the French Quarter year round. New Orleans is a city that stays warm enough that winter doesn't keep people away. Most people in the rest of Louisiana generally avoided coming to New Orleans unless they had to. Anna was wishing she was somewhere else too.

She was excited at the prospect of seeing Pierce. This had been put off long enough. Would she actually see him this time? What would that entail? Had he been tortured? Would he be angry that she had brought his mother into this danger? Her stomach was churning and she felt acid rise in her throat. Her knees began to shake. She wasn't cut out for this sort of thing. She began to silently pray as she saw the club where they were intended to make the exchange. She felt like she was stepping off a cliff.

Chapter Thirty-Two

Trais jumped on his bicycle and hurried down to the pier. He hadn't brought a car because he wanted to look like a common local, which is what he had been for most of his life. After the nice Acura he tooled around New Orleans in, this bike was slightly humiliating... but anything for the job.

His legs pumped on the pedals as fast as he could make them. At least he was getting his workout even without the advantage of the fancy gym he had joined. There was the boat, thankfully still tied to the pier instead of out in the gulf. Trais skidded to a stop and unceremoniously dropped the bike in the dust as he ran up to the craft.

"Dad! Dad! Where are you?"

"I'm right here, son." His dad was hitching up his overalls as he walked out of the cabin. "What's the emergency?"

"Dad, I was trying to help out my friend, Pierce. Some really bad dudes have him held hostage. We've got to get to New Orleans and get the police to look for him. I don't think I can handle this on my own any more."

"I didn't get a chance to tell you, but a police detective came by earlier with some information about you and your chef friend. I told him I would help him find your friend as long as it kept you out of danger."

"I know. You did the right thing, Dad. I should have known I could trust you. Now we've got to get to New Orleans! We've got to find the detective. Pierce and the men who had him are gone and I don't know where. They didn't say anything. They just left!" Trais was getting out of breath in his panic.

"Hold on, son. I've got my car in the usual place. I'll take you to New Orleans and we can find the detective."

"But are you sure we can trust him?"

"I usually consider myself a pretty good judge of character, though it seems I might have misjudged my own son. I do think this cop can be trusted. If not, I'll handle him."

Trais gave his dad a look of respect before they turned and hurried the couple of blocks to the car. They left a cloud of dust behind them. They also left the bicycle lying on the ground at the pier. They didn't give it a thought.

Chapter Thirty-Three

Anna saw the strip club up ahead. There were men spilled out on the sidewalk waiting to get in. It must be one of the more popular places; maybe the girls here were actually a tad attractive. Most of the women at these strip joints were strung out on drugs with their bodies showing the ravages of their addiction: sagging skin, wrinkled faces, blotchy complexions, missing teeth, and sometimes numerous sores. She would never be able to understand why people paid money to interact with them.

She headed toward the door with determination. Then, she checked the address again just to be sure. It was with some relief that she saw that this was not the correct address; instead, it was the unassuming club further up. It looked like all it served was liquor and music. She let out a sigh of relief as she pushed the chair containing her precious friend toward the danger.

As Anna tried to push Edith through the narrow entrance, she was met with a door that had such a strong spring load that it was difficult to hold it open while managing the wheelchair. The building was so old that the threshold looked like it had been created by ancient, bumpy cobblestones.

She gave up trying to go in frontward and turned the chair around so that the over-sized back wheels could ride over the overly bulky, jagged mound where the smaller, front wheels couldn't travel. It was still a struggle to keep the door open long enough to get the chair through before it slammed shut on the footrests.

"Park us at the front," Edith instructed.

"Why?" Anna questioned. "I thought you were supposed to sit at the back up against the wall so that you could see everything going on."

"Typically, that would be the case, but I don't want them having time to scrutinize my face and notice the deception."

"Ah. Makes sense." Anna was learning as she went along and making sure to store all the information for future use. She realized that Edith, now in her Trident mode, was scoping out the vacationing crowd and making mental notes about exits and escape routes.

There was a three-man jazz band on the slightly elevated platform at the front with seats placed around cocktail sized tables. Everyone seemed to be drinking copiously and enjoying the music more with each drink. People were clapping and swaying with the rhythm.

One couple had made an impromptu clearing between tables where they were dancing as if no one were around, meaning very erotically. It was Bourbon Street. It was expected.

Most of the tables were filled, but Anna saw one that contained only two women who were holding hands.

There was, surprisingly, some extra room at their table next to the stage, so Anna asked if they could join them.

"Why sure! We'd be happy to share! Hey," the tall elegant lady called to a passing server. "Drinks for our new friends. Put it on my tab."

"Oh, that's not necessary." Anna quickly spoke up. "We appreciate it, but we're meeting some people here. Maybe just a couple of glasses of ice water?"

The skeletal server nodded her head and slinked away. Anna didn't know if she'd come back with the drinks or not. She seemed to be in a sort of a daze and probably knew that water wouldn't bring much of a tip. It didn't matter.

Anna tried not to keep looking at her phone. Their contact was fifteen minutes late, twenty minutes late. She started getting antsy. Edith reached over and grabbed her hand to still her. Now the table contained two couples of ladies clasping hands.

Holding Edith's hand provided a calming influence. "Hang tight, girl. They'll be here. In fact, they probably already are, and currently observing us. They will find it perfectly normal for you to be holding my hand since they think I'm your mother and that you'll be giving me up for your lover soon."

"Do you think that's what they believe?"

"I would if I were in their position."

"Is that a good thing or a bad thing?"

"We'll know soon enough."

Two men at the back of the room started laughing and talking about their drunk friend who was hanging limply between them. It drew Anna's attention so she couldn't help looking back. She immediately sucked in her breath.

"Steady girl," cautioned Trident. "Don't react."

How could she ever think she might not recognize Pierce after all these years? Even with his fairly long dark brown hair hung over his face in sweaty strands, she knew him instantly. His head lolled around on his neck and his eyes seemed like they were trying to focus. She knew it the instant they locked on her before again sliding away uncontrollably. He still cared. She didn't know what they had done to him. She began to silently pray as she turned her head back toward the stage. "It's them," she whispered to her aunt.

"I know."

Anna gazed at her aunt. How could she be so calm? That was her son dangling between a couple of murderers. Edith was taking in slow, even breaths, but Anna comprehended, upon closer scrutiny, that she was like a tiger on the prowl ready to pounce. Anna gripped her hand harder and felt Edith grip back. Anna knew that she was praying too.

The sound of scraping chairs was behind them. Anna stole a look, just like any normal person would. She saw that the men had moved the chairs up right behind them and settled in so closely that their knees hit them in the back. People behind them started complaining and yelling that they were blocking their view. The tall man on Pierce's left looked back and said, in a tone that allowed no argument, "You're listening, not watching. Stick to your own business." The out-of-towner feared that he was up against something he wasn't used to. He and his slightly plump wife decided it was time to move on to other Bourbon Street entertainments. It felt like others in the audience were shifting out of the way as much as possible in the confined space. Then she felt the hand come up from behind and tightly grip her shoulder.

She winced as the pressure was increased, and bit her lip to keep from crying out. The pressure of Edith's hand increased as well, giving her the reassurance she needed. "Do you want this bum I've got doped up sitting next to me or do you prefer to keep your used-up old mother in the wheelchair? She doesn't look like she's got long to live, if you ask me. I think you're getting the better end of this deal."

"Would you give up your mother?" Anna whispered back.

"Ha! In an instant! Especially for what they're paying me."

"Well, I feel sorry for you that you didn't have a mother that you cared about."

"She never cared about me, so why should I?" Liam sneered.

"Surely your mother cared for you!"

"What do you know! Mind your own business!"

Anna could tell that the man was getting upset. She glanced at Edith who shook her head very slightly trying to let her know that this wasn't a good tactic. She couldn't seem to stop herself. "You look like a decent, even handsome man. I can't imagine any mother not being proud to call you her son. Don't you have an aunt or granny or anyone who loves you?"

"I'm not here for a counseling session. I'm here to handle some business. Now, I'm going to leave this drunk sitting here in his seat, and my friend and I will take control of that wheelchair you've been pushing."

At this, Anna turned around and stared the depraved man in the eye. "How dare you threaten my mother! What kind of a monster are you, anyway?"

Liam slowly withdrew the revolver from his pocket. "This kind," he answered.

Anna's eyes grew wide and her breath escaped her. She felt like she was completely frozen. Liam and his companion stood up. When they did, Pierce slowly slumped over onto the chair next to him. Liam took hold of the wheelchair and turned it toward the door. The conversation with Anna had gotten him so upset he didn't even look at Edith's face.

"No!" Anna whispered. She felt her strangled voice fighting to be heard.

Liam directed the wheelchair on the same path through the crowd that they had made when they came in. Edith sat there with a nearly imperceptible smirk on her face.

As they got to the door, Liam's partner held it open for him to bring the chair through. Liam tried. He pushed and pushed while the front wheels twisted and stuck on the poorly formed threshold. Finally, his partner squeezed around the back of the chair, adding his assistance to get their prisoner through.

"What's wrong with this stupid thing?" man number two questioned.

"I don't know. Maybe they rigged it somehow. I'm not some kind of wheelchair expert!" Liam growled.

While the two of them were distracted and trapped in the narrow doorway behind the chair, Edith heaved out of the chair and bolted away. The chair was lodged in place so the men had to pull it back out of the way before they could take off after Edith. As soon as they were outside the door, it occurred to them that they had left their bait inside with Anna.

"You go catch the old woman, and I'll go back in for our prisoner."

When Liam reentered the club, he saw Anna crying and pulling on Pierce. "Wake up! Get up, Pierce! We've got to get out of here!" she pleaded. He was struggling to stand up and Anna was using all her strength to try to help him. She was looking around frantically for someone to assist her but no one was aware of the danger. They just thought her date had had too much to drink. Then, she saw Liam walking toward them. She redoubled her efforts pulling and screaming at Pierce.

Liam walked up and placed his hand on her shoulder again with the same kind of intense pressure he had used on her previously. She felt paralyzed by it and let go of Pierce. When Liam analyzed the situation, he decided on his course of action. Pierce was left lying on the floor and

Anna felt the gun in her ribs as Liam's arm encircled her. She experienced a sudden calm come over her heart. She held her head up high and walked beside her captor out of the door. Her purse was underneath Pierce on the floor. The jazz band continued to play without missing a beat.

Chapter Thirty-Four

Through long years of training and experience, Edith knew the importance of keeping cash in her pocket. She quickly handed the adequate bill to the cabbie and worked her ample frame out of the back seat. Though it was late, she saw a light still on in the hotel room adjacent to hers. She knew never to carry anything that might identify her, even her hotel room key card.

Doctor Karns had been waiting up for their return. At her knock on the door, he abruptly opened it. He looked up at her from his wheelchair and asked the question she had been dreading. "Where's Anna?"

"I don't know. I hope my fleeing the scene gave her enough time and diversion to get out of there."

"So all we can do is wait?"

"That's it. We wait." Edith's eyes then took in the hotel room. Pelican was lying in her bed sleeping. The area had accumulated so much junk and mess that Edith couldn't understand how it could get this bad in so short a time. "Phil, the room! What happened?"

"You know Pelican. She's not comfortable unless she makes her little nest of debris. I tried to tidy up a bit and she went into a tizzy. I figured it's just better to leave things the way she wants them. I keep the *Do Not Disturb* sign on the door so housekeeping doesn't come messing around in here and get her upset."

"Yep. She's always been that way. Everyone has their own coping mechanism. Hers has always been clutter."

Edith opened the door into her room and invited the doctor to join her there as they waited for Anna and Pierce to return.

"They must be taking precautions before coming back. Or maybe they want some time to themselves to get reacquainted after such a long separation. It will probably take them a while to get here. We can just sit and catch up on the good ol' days as we wait."

"Well, a lot of water has run under the bridge since we last visited. It seems the only time I ever saw you was when someone was injured. I guess our first contact was back when you and Pelican were new assets. I had been the contract doctor for several years at that time. The money was good and the cause was something that gave my life special meaning after the death of my young wife. The first time I laid eyes on Pellie, I fell for her."

"Yes. I know. The feeling there was mutual, but you both knew that The Cooking School wouldn't allow it."

"We got around that very cleverly, didn't we? Her marriage to a man who was also looking to cover his lifestyle, which, at the time, was what folks did. It worked out well for all of us."

"And Anna still doesn't know?"

"She doesn't. I don't think it would be best to tell her."

"All three of them, right?" questioned Edith.

"Of course. Pelican was always faithful. I never thought I could love again until she came along. I'm so glad to have this time with her, even under these circumstances. You've heard the poem by Robert Browning, 'Come grow old with me. The best is yet to be'."

Edith smiled at the sentiment. "So, you didn't have any difficulties with the organization when you were put into a home?"

"Why should I? I wasn't privy to any real secrets, just the use of my medical practice to stitch some strangers up. What's to know about that? Besides, my mental faculties are all still fully functional. I know how to conduct myself. My poor Pellie doesn't. It breaks my heart to see her like this. My hope and prayer is that I can look after her from now on. Can you try to work that into the rest of the plans you're making, please, Trident?"

"I'll do my very best. In fact, I'll make it a priority."

"That's more than I can hope. You've made this old man very happy. Thank you."

Chapter Thirty-Five

Trais and his dad hurried into the police station. "We need to see Detective MacGregor," Trais told the policeman at the desk.

"He's not here. I'll get someone else for you."

"No. I can't talk to someone else. I'm his um… some kind of informant, um… yeah! Confidential! I'm his confidential informant." Trais straightened his back and declared, "I'm Detective MacGregor's CI and I have some information he needs right now!"

Mr Fuqua looked at his son and shook his head. "Boy, you've been watching too much TV. Give me your name and I'll contact him."

"Trais Fuqua is my name and this is my dad, Roger Fuqua."

"OK. If you two will just take a seat, I'll see what I can do. It might take a while though."

Trais was feeling impatient but knew it wouldn't do any good to show it. This was the best they could hope for, he thought, as they sat down in the uncomfortable, stained, plastic seats.

After about a half an hour, a detective walked up to them and asked them to come back to his office. As they entered, Trais noticed that it contained two desks. He was pretty sure that one of them belonged to MacGregor. "I'm Detective Brown, Detective MacGregor's partner. Anything you need to tell him, you can tell me."

Mr Fuqua was trying to determine the best way to handle this. "Do you like to fish, Detective?"

"Does that have something to do with all this?" Brown asked.

"In a way, it kinda does. You see, I own a shrimp boat that docks down at Cocodrie. Have you ever been down da bayou to Cocodrie?"

"As a matter of fact, I have. Are y'all getting any red fish out of the bayou? They were protected from commercial fishing for a while since they had been over-fished. They're the best tasting fish you can eat."

"They're still protected commercially, but hobby fishermen can pull them out on a line and enjoy them. My boy Trais here is a top-notch cook. I've never tasted anything as good as when he cooks up a red fish."

Trais looked at his dad, surprised at the compliment. "Yeah, Detective. Come on down soon and we'll regale you with fish, and perhaps, information."

"What kind of information might I be interested in?"

"It's pretty complicated," Trais explained, hoping he wasn't giving too much away. "A friend of mine was recently kidnapped."

A light bulb went on over Detective Brown's head. "A friend of yours? He wouldn't by chance own a restaurant, would he?

"Well..." Trais hedged as the door opened. He stopped speaking instantly as he saw Pierce being pushed in a wheelchair through the door. MacGregor made sure not to register recognition toward Trais or his dad, but just plopped a lady's purse on his desk. Pierce looked like he was trying to shake some cobwebs from his head. Trais knew the look. He'd seen it enough times when he was on the street.

Chapter Thirty-Six

They hadn't bothered to drug Anna. She seemed docile enough for them to handle without the need. She was trying to get comfortable on the big bed in the beautiful room. It wasn't easy with the cuffs and chains, but it was late and she was so terribly tired. It had been a grueling experience. She fell asleep praying, trusting and allowing God's comfort to fill her heart.

The next morning, she woke up to the smell of coffee and bacon. The young man placing the tray at her bedside said, "Hello, Anna. My name is Trais."

"You know me?" Anna struggled into a sitting position and reached for her coffee.

"I know of you. Don't be afraid."

She looked at him steadily. "I'm not afraid. I know that God has everything under control."

"Okaaaay." Trais stretched out the word thinking, *This lady must be delusional or crazy. I probably can't trust her enough to tell her anything.* "Well, I hope you enjoy your breakfast," he said, backing out of the room.

As Anna was finishing up the last bite of her breakfast, Liam entered the room. He stood observing her for a moment. "I've never seen anyone chained to a bed who has such an appetite. Aren't you worried that I'm going to kill you?"

"First, how many people have you seen chained to a bed?"

"Quite a few as a matter of fact."

"Hmmmm," was all Anna responded.

"Well, let me introduce myself. My name is Liam. You can call me Liam." At this he seemed amused at himself and started to chuckle.

"My name is Anna Hubbard." She extended her hand the way she usually did when introducing herself. Liam just looked at it in surprise. She slowly laid it back in her lap.

"Hubbard, huh? Like the old mother?"

Anna smiled. "I get that a lot."

"Why are you sitting there smiling! Don't you comprehend the danger you're in?"

"But I'm not in any danger, Liam. The worst you can do is kill me and then I'll just go and be with my Lord."

"You sound just like my old granny did. I always thought she was crazy."

"I never met her but she certainly doesn't sound crazy to me. Is she still living?

"No."

"I'm sure she prayed for you a great deal, Liam."

"Well, if she did, she was wasting her time."

"It's never too late."

"Lady, you don't know what you're talking about."

"Actually, I do. Once there was a man named Saul who hated the followers of Christ so much that he went around killing them and putting them in prison. The Savior came to him and forgave him. He became one of the greatest missionary evangelists of his time. Do you recognize these names? Romans, Corinthians, Ephesians?"

"They're familiar."

"God used Saul, who changed his name to Paul, to pen several books of the Bible. Now, would He use someone who was a murderer to do something like that?"

"I don't guess so. How should I know?" he answered gruffly.

"But when he turned to the Savior, his sins were washed away and he was no longer a murderer. If God could do that for him, He can do it for anyone. You too."

Liam started to twitch uncomfortably. "Lady, I'm glad you've got religion. You're going to need it. I didn't manage to trade that chef for my mark, but I'll get it done with you."

"Why would you want to kill a little old lady?"

"At first it was just the job, but then she killed my friend. He was more than a friend. He was my cousin. His mama raised me after mine ran off. I don't know why the hell I'm telling you this!"

Anna winced at his mild expletive. "Liam, my mama didn't kill your cousin. She startled him at the top of the stairs and he fell. It was an accident."

"Ha! Likely story! A little old lady scaring a man so much that he falls down the steps and cracks his head open!"

"My mother can be very scary."

Liam examined Anna's open features for a moment and then said, "Enjoy your stay, Anna." He closed the door loudly behind him.

Chapter Thirty-Seven

$\mathcal{D}$etective MacGregor said goodbye to Trais and his dad before he returned his attention to Anna's purse. He rummaged through and pulled out her wallet. After extracting her credit cards, he left the room for a moment. When he returned, he announced, "Hopefully tracing the cards will provide us a good lead."

It didn't take long before a uniformed officer returned with a computer print-out. He looked at Pierce and said, "Do you know an Anna Hubbard?"

"Yes. She's my cousin," Pierce knew that wasn't factually true, but it was close enough for now.

"Good. You're coming with us."

Officer Brown asked, "Do you mind telling me what's going on?

"It's complicated," was the only answer MacGregor was willing to give just yet. "Would you mind just playing along for now?" He knew how much Officer Brown enjoyed showing off his authority, so it would be difficult for him to walk into anything blind. MacGregor hoped that their year on the job together was enough to develop the level of trust he needed.

It was after midnight before they pulled up at the hotel. Officer Brown was given the task of flashing his badge and finding out the room number. Maybe giving him something he deemed important to do would keep him placated for the time being.

Brown jumped back into the car and said, "They've got two rooms. They're around back." He drove the car and parked in the parking lot next to an old conversion van that looked like it had traveled many miles of rough road. The light was on in one of the designated rooms so that was the one they knocked on. "New Orleans police, open the door," Officer Brown barked as MacGregor rolled his eyes. *Was that really necessary?* he thought.

The door was opened by an elderly lady with a worried look on her face. She showed that she had nothing to hide by opening it as wide as she could so they could see the elderly man in the wheelchair behind her. She knew that opening it only slightly would start the conversation off wrong, which was the last thing she wanted to do. She needed to find out about Anna.

"Ma'am, I have a man in the squad car who says he could find his cousin here," MacGregor told her.

"Pierce!" she yelled. "You have Pierce? Thank God! I'm his mother. Do you have Anna too?"

This wasn't what the officers were expecting. "Someone else is missing?" asked Officer Brown.

Edith was running out to the car with MacGregor following. Pierce had shaken off his drug-induced stupor enough by now to get out of the car by himself and give his mother a long hug. She clung to him. "Oh, Pierce! I thought you were dead. I thought I had killed you!"

"Shush now, Mother. I'm fine. You've done nothing wrong."

The officers were taking in her words. Why would she think that she had killed her son? And why was his cousin now apparently missing? There was way more going on here than they were able to figure out… yet.

Edith drew Pierce into the room with the detectives following closely behind. Pierce looked questioningly at the doctor.

"This is D Karns, an old friend of your Aunt Pelle," explained Edith. "She's in the next room sleeping so could we try to keep things a bit quiet?"

It was too late; screaming and moaning could be heard through the closed door connecting the two rooms. "What's wrong with her?" asked Pierce as he hurried to open the door."

"Pierce, she has Alzheimer's. I'm afraid her mind is going. She might be upset if you go to her. She probably won't know you. I'll take care of her."

"Let me go," Doctor Karns said. "I've been doing well with her now that she's been able to place me."

Edith watched him as he used his legs to scoot the chair forward and through the door. She knew he preferred not to be helped unless he asked for it. It was hard to watch him struggle, but she couldn't resist admiring him.

Pierce noticed the strange look on her face. "Mom?"

She just shook her head. "Long story. Now, could everyone find a seat and let's see if we can figure this out together?"

MacGregor sat there looking at the group in the room. Everyone had their secrets. He had recognized Anna as the woman he spoke to at the Goodwill store, and once inside the hotel, he recognized the rest of her group that had been shopping for clothes at the same time he was finding his outfit for the unsanctioned undercover operation.

He couldn't explain to himself why he chose to help in the way he had. He knew there was more to the whole situation than anyone was willing to say, including him. Experience told him that there were some in the New Orleans Police Force who didn't play by the rules. He didn't want to take any risks here. His foolish choices had lost him his own family, and now he was involved with two families, maybe more, who were trying to rescue each other from something. He just hadn't quite figured it out yet.

Though Pierce hadn't seen it happen, he knew that Anna had been taken in his place. He didn't know the exact location of the antebellum home he had been held in, but he knew it was in Cocodrie, and that was where Anna would most likely be.

Contact information was exchanged and backup meeting places were arranged. MacGregor assured them that he had a source who was close to where Anna probably was. They would all be kept apprised of the situation as events unfolded. He let them know that he was to meet with his source the following morning. Pierce knew that source was Trais, but he chose to keep that information to himself for the time being. It was the best any of them could do. They said their good nights.

Soon after the detectives left, Edith and Pierce were catching one another up on the events of the past several days when there was a soft tapping on the door. Edith peeked out and saw their new friends, the Haitians. She opened up and allowed them to slip inside. The number of people involved just kept growing. It gave Edith an uncomfortable feeling since everything she had ever known about espionage work was to not let anyone know what was going on.

This new family seemed to be expanding beyond her control, but they all seemed to care. She now had someone who she knew cared more than anyone, so she silently bowed her head to Him.

Chapter Thirty-Eight

They called him Number Two. People who weren't in the know assumed that it was because he was subordinate to Liam. That particular misunderstanding served his purposes. He was the head agent of The Cooking School in Quebec. The cover there was a hunting lodge supplying guides for rich people on moose or caribou hunts. He got his nickname for a far different reason than that he was subordinate to anyone. When people actually got to know him, he scared the 'number two' out of them.

Years before, he had been in love with a Russian agent. His love for her was so deep that he would do anything to please her, even to the point of treason toward the confederation of world powers that tried to promote freedom. Freedom meant nothing to him, only Tasha. He never admitted to the term 'double agent' but that was essentially what he was. No one knew his secret, and he thought he was safe, until a nosey operative known as the Pelican looked into his business. When Tasha disappeared, he put out feelers all over the world to try to find her.

Pelican came to him to make a deal. She would protect Tasha and his secret, but he was never to see her again. She thought the work they were doing was too important for it to get a black eye over a misguided love affair. Soon afterward, he learned that Tasha had been imprisoned in Russia. She was never heard from again. He appreciated too well the fate of any Russian suspected of fraternizing with the enemy.

His blood boiled every time he thought of it. He had long sought revenge, and then the opportunity was dropped into his lap. Others who didn't know better might not recognize her, but he could never forget her. Pelican had been able to sweet-talk the Mexicans and the Haitians, according to information on The Cooking School site, but he would never stop until she was dead. He didn't care if she was an old woman who didn't know her own name any more. He didn't know the identity of the young woman in the next room, but he felt certain that she was the key to getting what he wanted. Liam was spending a good deal of time chatting her up. Maybe it would prove valuable.

***

Trais was in the kitchen preparing dinner when Liam walked in. "What are you cooking?"

"Well, I had to fall back on what was in the freezer, so I'm just making a roast. Y'all are basically British, right? Wouldn't you like a nice Yorkshire pudding? It will make you feel like you're at home out here on this Louisiana bayou."

"A roast might be a nice change, but I think Number Two has been hung up on seafood every day since he's soaking up the local culture."

"I didn't make it to the dock today. My bicycle is gone," Trais explained.

"Gone? What happened?'

"All I can figure is that someone must have stolen it."

Liam's eyebrows went up. "Stolen! That means someone was out here."

"I guess. All I know is that it isn't here any more and it takes too long to walk to the dock, so I'm fixing this roast."

"Hmmmm." As Liam walked away, he said, "I'll see what we can do. You might do me a favor and go look after our 'guest' while I check out the perimeter. Number Two is busy in his office catching up on some paperwork. I'm sure he'll find you more useful if you help out in more jobs around here than just in the kitchen."

Trais decided that this situation could go either way for him and the captive upstairs. He was feeling desperate for a solution to the problem of getting everyone out of this alive.

Chapter Thirty-Nine

The new little family group were all sitting around the hotel room planning whatever their next move might be. It felt like a game of chess to Pierce. He would figure out his next three moves and then his opponent would come out with the unexpected and none of his plans would work any more. His mind was working furiously as his eyes took in those gathered in the room. The Haitians were Manny and John, well-trained, fit and capable. Then there were his mom and him, well trained, but with his mom not so fit any more, and the two elderly people, whom Pierce considered to be pure liabilities when it came to any type of operation. And then there was Anna, untrained, innocent and held captive by people who would murder her if they felt it was necessary. Pierce decided it was the worst day of his life.

He shook himself out of his morose thoughts to hear what the others were saying.

Edith was trying to explain to Aunt Pelle why she wouldn't be allowed to participate in the operation to retrieve her daughter. She knew that Pelican wouldn't admit to having Alzheimer's, so she decided on another tack. "Dear, you know how bad your arthritis has gotten. You can't do what you used to do."

Pelican turned an angry expression on Trident and said, "You don't know what you're talking about! I don't have arthritis! You don't know anything about me!"

Edith was surprised by her not even admitting to arthritis and tried to mollify her. "I'm sorry. I thought you had arthritis."

"What do you know?! You don't know me. I'll bet you don't even know where I was born."

This was information her long-time partner did know about her so she answered, "You were born in Miami, Florida."

Pelican looked placated and answered, "Oh! Well, I guess you do know me. I am going to help though, and you can't stop me. What is the operation?"

Pierce looked at the Haitians. They exchanged very worried looks. This was not going to be easy.

"I think we need to find another place to stay. This has been compromised. I have an idea," Pierce said. "Mom, can I take the van for a little while?

"Of course, son. Anything you need," his mother answered.

***

Pierce pulled the van up to the front door of The Good Shepherd Homeless Shelter. Todd peeked out and then threw the door open. "I'm so glad to see you in one piece… um… what's your name! Ha!"

Pierce smiled at the perpetually cheerful man. "Yeah. It was a bit of a mess, but I got it straightened out. Do you still have my bag here?"

"No. I'm sorry. The police took it. They haven't concluded their investigation into the death in the church."

"You're not implicated, are you?"

"I don't think so, it's just red tape."

"That's OK. I guess everything in it can be replaced.

"What I could do with is a little help, if you're up to it."

"Always happy to help a good cook in need! What can I do for you?"

"I have three elderly folks who require a temporary place to stay. Do you have a way to accommodate them? There are two women and one man and it would be important for them to all stay together."

"Sure. We have a family wing available now. I could house them there for a short term."

Pierce let out a big sigh of relief. "That would be awesome! I'll do my best cooking if I know my loved ones are safe."

"Family's everything, isn't it?" asked Todd.

"It sure is."

Todd smiled, knowing that he was making good on his promise to himself to help Pierce if the opportunity were ever presented to him. That was what made Todd the happiest, helping those in need. He knew that the most effective way of doing that would be to share the gospel. He silently prayed that God would give him the opportunity.

Chapter Forty

Trais tapped hesitantly on Anna's door.

"Come in," she answered with a question in her tone. She never knew what was coming next. She had never seen Trais without food in his hands, and when he came in this time, he didn't disappoint.

"I thought you might like a little snack. I made some lemon doberge cake." He entered the room with cake and coffee while leaving the door slightly ajar.

Anna's eyes lit up. "How did you know? It's my favorite!" She struggled more than the action required to sit up on the bed to savor her cake. "Could you loosen these chains so I can properly enjoy my treat?"

Trais wanted to be helpful anyway, so he managed to lift a corner of the heavy iron bed up enough to slip the end of the chain out from under it. Her hands and feet were still shackled, but she had more freedom of movement. The tray was placed on the bedside table. She expected Trais to leave the room as he usually did. He didn't leave; but she figured this would be her only opportunity. "I really hate to waste good cake," she said as she swung the heavy serving tray at Trais' head.

She was darting out the door as Trais hit the floor. She made more noise than she wanted with the jingling of the chains, and her steps were restricted, so she chose to slide down the banister like she had done as a child. She popped off at the end right by the front door and darted out onto the porch directly into the broad, stony chest of Liam.

Trais collided with both of them from her back before she had a chance to catch her breath. With the double whammy, Liam stepped back to balance himself. When he did, he brought the whole group down the steps to land in the spongy Louisiana soil.

Number Two was stepping out the front door as they were trying to disentangle limbs and chains. He stepped up and grabbed the loop in between Anna's wrists and dragged her back up the stairs. Liam and Trais heard the slaps and screams through the closed door. They were standing in the hall as Two slammed out of her room. He was so angry that neither of the men dared to speak to him. They stood in stunned silence.

It had been agreed upon that the hostage would not be harmed. Two was obviously losing patience. Presently they heard something from behind the door where they knew an injured Anna was lying. Her voice was sweetly singing:

"Lord I would place my hand in thine,
Nor ever murmur nor repine,
Content whatever lot I see,
For 'tis thy hand that leadeth me.

He leadeth me, He leadeth me,
By His own hand He leadeth me,
His faithful follower I would be,
For 'tis His hand that leadeth me."

Trais looked aghast. "That crazy religious lunatic tried to brain me and now she's singing! I've never seen such a thing in my life!" He walked away shaking his head. He didn't notice the tears streaming down Liam's face.

Anna fell into an exhausted sleep, even though her body protested from multiple bruises and what she hoped was only a sprained, rather than a broken, wrist. In her dream, she continued to sing the song that had brought her comfort after the terror of the confrontation with the angry Canadian man, who had seldom spoken or interacted with her previously.

She was in a rocking chair on the porch of the beautiful mansion she currently occupied. In her arms was the tiny baby she had lost in that neonatal unit so many years ago. The wrinkled little face of her only child was something she tried hard not to dwell on. The pain was still acute after over ten years. In her dream, she spoke to the fragile infant. "Yes, my love. Mommy will see you again. I don't know if it will be today or if it will be many years, but I will see you again." She didn't realize that her tears were wetting her pillow in her sleep.

Chapter Forty-One

Pierce had gotten his charges settled in their new living space, not glamorous but comfortable, when there was a knock on the outside door. He opened it to two smiling men, Manny and John. "May we come in, zanmi?" they asked using Creole slang.

Edith looked up. "Do you have our guns and ammo?"

"No fear, manman. Everything is safe. It will be available at the precise moment you need it."

"Have you been able to find out anything?" Pierce wondered.

"New recipes are being created. The people who have Anna are hard at work making sure that they provide the information we need using a series of recipes. It looks like they are planning a complicated water trade off. The details are still in the works. We also have been coordinating from our end."

"I've got to get my car out of the police impound. They said I could get it today. I have a little trip to take."

"Come on. We'll take you there. You'll have to walk the last few blocks because, well, I would prefer not to be connected."

"Say no more. Thanks for all your help. Are you still staying in the same hotel?"

"We decided that a strategic move was in order. We're now in a lovely little out of the way bed and breakfast. They were fine with taking our cash." Manny smiled.

"I'm sure they were! OK. Let's go. Mom, y'all sit tight. I'll be back in time to fix supper for everyone. Love you!" Edith's heart swelled with love and pride for her son.

***

What was it about the feel of his own car? The familiarity of how the seat conformed to his shape and the alignment of his controls produced in him a sense of security. The police had checked it out and were impressed at the extra power he had paid a mechanic to provide under the Camry's hood.

He liked the nondescript car. It suited him. It cruised the two hours down to Cocodrie without a glitch. There was the shrimp boat right where he expected it to be at the end of the pier. He brought the car to a stop in the dirt and let his athletic body transport his fine-tuned brain onto the boat where he was expecting to figure out what to do. He needed to talk to Trais, but the only one on the boat was Mr Fuqua.

"Could we have a little chat, Mr Fuqua?"

"About what?"

"About Trais and how valuable he is to the security of our nation." If he had wanted to surprise the man, he couldn't have done a better job than what his words had just accomplished.

"Just who are you really?" the fisherman asked suspiciously.

"I'm the one who has been looking after your son and teaching him my trade."

"I know who you are. I saw you at the police station, but really, who are you besides being a chef? You are a chef, aren't you?"

"That and more. Let's go where we can have some privacy."

At the end of the conversation, Mr Fuqua's head was spinning and his emotions were raw. How could he have misjudged his son so completely? He had always seen his intelligence and drive, but didn't realize that he had been unconsciously trying to channel it to his own benefit in his business. Trais needed so much more, and it seemed he had found it. Instead of having a third son who was a disappointment, he had a son he could have immense pride in, but wouldn't be able to share that pride with anyone. What he had just heard gave him bragging rights, but then, the information immediately took those rights away.

"So, Trais is a secret agent?"

"And a great chef."

"Oh my, my! If his momma was here, she'd give him a big hug and then tan his hide."

"Right now, people's lives are at stake, and Trais is the only one in a position to help save them."

"I don't want my boy in danger!"

"Sir, your son is a young man and has been in danger many times. It just so happens that you know about it this time. My sources are telling me that a prisoner exchange is planned over the water not far from here. Can we count on you for the use of your boat and on your expertise as a captain?"

Mr Fuqua stood tall and proud as he committed to do whatever was needed to help his son and his nation. When he learned that helpless — using the term loosely — elderly people were involved, he was even more adamant.

"There are a few more people I need to contact to get this operation lined up. We can't have any mistakes. I'll be in touch when I have more particulars. In the meantime, if Trais comes down to see you, just reassure him that we've got everything under control. I'm sure he's been quite worried thinking he's alone in all this."

On the drive back to New Orleans, Pierce was calculating the recipes and how he should code them to respond to the demands of the kidnappers. He was thinking of a shrimp dip and then calamari appetizer. The main dish should be something spectacular — something dramatic. He was sure that the dessert would have to be bananas foster. Flambé might be a necessary end to the meal.

Chapter Forty-Two

Detectives MacGregor and Brown had some rare down time and were sitting in their office shooting the breeze. MacGregor cleverly guided the conversation in the direction he wanted it to go. "Hey, Brown! I just got a great idea!"

"Oh yeah! What's that?"

"I've been thinking of all that talk about pulling some red fish out of the bayou down there in Cocodrie. You and I never do anything fun together, except for catching criminals. That's fun. Anyway, how about we plan a fishing trip?"

"That's not a bad idea. The wife thinks I should spend every minute I'm not at work hanging out with her and the kids. Don't get me wrong, I love my family, but now and then, a man needs some man time. You know?"

"I know exactly what you mean. I'll check with a guy I know and we'll firm up the plans when his boat is free. We'll split the cost so it shouldn't be too much."

"Sounds great! Just let me know. Since I'll be with a colleague, my wife will think it's work related," Brown said with a mischievous smile.

"And I thought you were always walking the straight and narrow. I'm learning new things about you every day, buddy."

"Yeah. That's the persona I try to display. It works well with impressing the bosses, especially the wife." They both had a hearty laugh.

***

Manny and John, being brought up on the island of Haiti, were not only knowledgeable about boats, they were more comfortable on the water than on land. They were browsing around the boating specialty store looking for what they needed. There they were, the Mae West vests. These were the kind used on airplanes in case of crashes in the water. The vests were so thin that they could go unnoticed underneath clothing, but once they hit the water, they inflated automatically so the wearer looked like... well... hence the name.

They picked up two of them, which was more than they figured they needed. The elderly lady they were buying them for might not have the presence of mind to use any flotation device that wasn't automatic. Still, it had the potential to be extremely dangerous.

Not just any boat would do for this operation. It had to be able to gain speed quickly and that might be difficult to come by. They had advertised their need on The Cooking School website and were currently waiting for someone to come through with an offer. Because the counter-op wasn't sanctioned, they hoped it wouldn't deplete their resources too badly. They were planning to recoup some of their expenses from the friends they were trying to save. Manny didn't want to contact his dad, but if necessary, that would be an avenue of revenue of last resort.

As he was thinking about how to get a boat, his phone dinged. It was from someone down in Houma, Louisiana who said he had a second-hand boat for sale for $10,495. It was a Wellcraft Scarab with a 7.4 liter engine and V8 with 454 horsepower.

"I'll give you an even ten grand, if it checks out. We can come see it and get it today."

The seller seemed happy to move the boat quickly. "When can you get here?"

"We'll be there in an hour and a half."

"Great! See ya then!"

Things were coming together. Manny hoped it would be smooth sailing, but life always tends to throw curve balls.

Chapter Forty-Three

Trais served the savory roast with the Yorkshire pudding and a side of steamed summer vegetables. He had bought them frozen since it wasn't quite summer, but his diners didn't know the difference. He had prepared the key lime pie dessert earlier and it was sitting in the refrigerator letting its ingredients mingle and firm up. He would turn the heavy cream, powdered sugar and a touch of vanilla into delicious homemade whipped cream that would top his dessert at the last moment before serving, transforming it from delicious to truly exceptional. He was a little sad that the Canadians didn't have the culinary sophistication to realize how wonderful his creations were, but that wasn't what he was here for anyway.

He had left the door between the kitchen and the dining room cracked about an inch, as he always did, hoping to catch a hint as to his employers' plans. Number Two was complaining about how they had only rented this mansion for a week, thinking that would be plenty of time. Now the Airbnb owners were notifying them that the maid would be in the day after tomorrow to clean up after they vacated. They would have to remove any trace of their activities by then. They didn't want to create any more notice by attempting to change plans. This would require that events wrap up quickly.

He complained that they had already spent more on this operation than it was worth, so they needed to finish up with as little expense as possible.

"But we need a boat," Liam reminded him.

"Yes, but it doesn't have to be a fancy boat. Just large enough for three people. When we trade out a young woman for an old one, it will only take a minute before the old one is finished off by my own hands and then her body can be dumped into the bayou. Our cook is from around here. Surely, he knows someone who can lend us a little outboard fishing boat that will serve our purposes. Trais!" Number two yelled.

Even though he was standing right by the door, Trais quietly crept to the other side of the kitchen before walking noisily toward the door to stick his head out. "Yes, sir? Are you ready for dessert?"

"In a minute. Do you know someone who has a small boat with an outboard motor we can borrow or rent real cheap?"

"My cousin has a bateau with a trawling motor. It's not very fast or powerful, but it's enough to get you around for a while. Are you finally going to enjoy our local attractions and do a little fishing?"

"Yeah, sure. That's the plan."

"When will you need it? Do you have fishing gear? I'm sure my cousin could provide all that for you."

"How much do you think he wants for everything?"

"Oh, probably around a hundred dollars will do it. He'll deliver it gassed up and with the gear on board. You'll have to bring your own beer."

"Sounds good. Will cash work?" Liam pulled a one-hundred-dollar bill out of his wallet and extended it toward Trais.

"When will you need it?"

"How about tomorrow about six p.m.?"

"A little night fishing? I'll make sure my cousin includes a battery-powered lantern. Sounds like a lot of fun. Do you want me to go along as a guide?" Trais was hoping they would agree to it so that he could be on hand to protect Anna. Even though he considered her a little crazy didn't mean she didn't deserve a hero, as Trais liked to consider himself — the advocate for the oppressed and downtrodden.

"No. We won't stray far from the pier. I think we'll be all right just the two of us."

"OK." Trais made sure not to show his disappointment. "I'll talk to my cousin and let you know definitely. Oh, remember, my bicycle is gone. Would you let me borrow your car?"

"Sure." Liam tossed him the keys. They didn't usually let anyone else drive their rental, but feeling the time pressure to get this over with, made them willing to bend their rules.

Chapter Forty-Four

Edith was sitting in their room at the homeless shelter enjoying some TV with her feet propped up on the ottoman in front of the easy chair. She really needed this breather. Pierce was cooking for everyone so they were enjoying exceptional meals that were both nutritious and perfectly balanced with seasonings and optimum temperature.

Doctor Karns didn't need his wheelchair except for times when he wasn't sure on his feet, so he was sitting on the couch. Although Pelican could support her weight slightly during transfers from one location to another, they found it easier to leave her in her wheelchair when they didn't have a strong younger person on hand to help.

The doctor was watching the mindless program with a slight smile of contentment on his face. Life was as good as it gets at eighty. He was comfortable, well-fed, and with the one he loved.

Pelican sat in her wheelchair with an angry look on her face. Edith knew that her anger was as a result of her confusion. It was sad, but she recognized that there was nothing anyone could do about it but try to take care of her needs as best they could. She was glad that Doctor Karns understood this. She let out a sigh of contentment. She knew that things were about to become hectic and dangerous, so she enjoyed the momentary respite even more.

Pierce walked into the room. "OK, I've cleaned up after breakfast and ordered Chinese takeout delivered here for you for lunch. I'm heading down the bayou to get an update on getting Anna back. It will be a few hours so I would recommend that you all take a nap after lunch. Things could be coming to a head very soon. Love y'all," he said as he hugged his mom and his fake aunt, and then solemnly shook the doctor's hand.

They exchanged a long look that the doctor understood to mean he was to protect the ladies. He reached between the couch cushions and let his hand touch the loaded 38 S&W revolver. This was another reason they didn't trouble to place Pelican on the couch beside him. Her mental state made her contact with a firearm a most dangerous prospect.

***

Pierce pulled up to the pier where the boat for the Fuqua Shrimping Company was tied. Mr Fuqua was standing on the deck of his boat munching on a juicy mango as the dripping fruit left traces down the front of his overalls. Pierce couldn't help but admire the man's raw enjoyment of the mango's unique flavor, which he considered to be a cross between peach and cantaloupe with an added citrusy pop. Pierce tended to look at most of life as filled with one sort of flavor or another.

"Hi, Mr Fuqua. Have you seen Trais lately?"

"He just left."

"Oh." Pierce looked crestfallen. He had hoped to see his friend again. "Well, it's actually you I need to speak with."

Mr Fuqua was a man of few words, but the raising of his most active eyebrow asked the question for him.

"I don't know how much you know about all the trouble we've had going on…"

"Enough."

"OK. Then, without giving too many details, would you consider taking on a few passengers for a possibly dangerous excursion?"

"Possibly. Is it for a good cause?"

"The best! I'll give you whatever you require to make up for all your lost time shrimping. It's just that important. Additionally, I'll need you to allow me to help you make a small, reversible adaptation to a component of your boat."

"Reversible? So, it won't mess anything up?"

"Not at all."

"OK then. Long as the money's good and the cause is good. When do you need it?"

"It should take less than an hour to hook up the modification and then I'll be back by about five-thirty at the latest."

"You'd better get a move on then," Mr Fuqua said, glancing at the Rolex Oyster he wore when he wasn't out to sea. The Oyster was the least expensive watch Rolex made, but what else would a moderately successful fisherman wear?

Chapter Forty-Five

Manny and John had to do some additional negotiating with the boat owner because he was trying to charge extra for the boat trailer.

"A boat trailer goes with the boat! You don't need a boat trailer without the boat and I can't take the boat without the trailer. What am I supposed to do, drive down the road in a boat? I've got to get it to Dulac to enter the gulf." Manny was trying not to let on how crucial his need was. "Look. I've got ten thousand cash right now. Take it or leave it!"

"So you weren't foolin' when you said cash?"

"Yes! Cash!"

The man got a big smile on his face. "That means my ex-wife won't know how much I got for it. Ha! Deal!"

The two men shook hands while John backed the truck up to the trailer before anyone changed their minds.

They were on the road to Dulac within fifteen minutes. They would be at the boat ramp in less than thirty minutes and could be heading up the canal toward Cocodrie about an hour after that, leaving extra time for safe navigation. This whole operation was a long way from over, but at least he'd be able to look his dad in the eye knowing he had done the right thing by their relatives. *Family is always the most important thing in life,* he thought as they headed down the highway full of bumps and ruts. Maybe they would have the boat in the water in forty-five minutes. Manny swallowed hard, knowing that they were cutting their time very close.

***

After the two men worked together to connect the necessary apparatus to the trawling beam, Pierce was heading back to New Orleans as quickly as he dared. The Google app on his phone notified him about speed traps but couldn't always be trusted for accuracy. In his desperation, he decided to try out that praying thing again. There was so much at stake. They couldn't be late.

***

Detectives Brown and MacGregor forked over the $200 for the use of the fishing boat. They were enjoying the whole prospect, though Brown was completely unaware that this was anything but a leisurely excursion. MacGregor tried to hide his anxiety from his partner, which was hard to do since they spent so much time together. He kept looking at the sky, worrying about the rain clouds gathering on the far horizon over the gulf, hoping they would hold off for a few hours.

"Oh, don't worry about rain, Mac! So what if we get a little wet. Here, have a beer."

MacGregor reached out and took the cold, dripping can, knowing he would only sip a little for appearance's sake. He needed all his wits about him if the exchange Pierce had carefully planned ran into any problems. He was to stay back and observe only, but he had not been filled in on the minute points.

Oh well. You couldn't force people to trust you. He just hoped that someday he would be given more particulars. This whole thing had been rather enigmatic. As a law enforcement officer, he didn't like enigmas. He liked facts and information.

Chapter Forty-Six

Anna lay on the bed with her left hand clutched to her chest. She was reasonably sure the tiny bones were broken since there were points sticking up where they shouldn't be. Shortly after Number Two had left her, Liam entered the room and looked her over. When he saw how rapidly her wrist was swelling, he had the good sense to remove that handcuff.

"You aren't going to try to take off again, are you?"

"No. I won't. I promise."

"OK. Try to get some rest. You'll be going home soon."

"But what about my mama?" she asked, with tears welling in her eyes.

"Ah! Your mama! I figured that must be the relationship. Don't worry. I'll do my best for her."

"But why don't you just call this whole business off? You are in charge, aren't you?

"Things aren't always as they appear. You just keep on praying."

Anna watched as Liam left the room. Then she began to smile knowing that the Lord was working on his heart.

She would never have come into contact with Liam had events not unfolded just as they had.

Perhaps God, who is powerful and sovereign, orchestrated all these circumstances just so she could share the gospel with Liam. *Wow,* she thought. *God never ceases to amaze.*

She turned over and shifted around on the comfortable bed, trying to ease the pain in her wrist so she could get a little sleep.

She must have dozed off because the sun was much lower in the sky and starting to cast long shadows of the moss-laden trees across the manicured lawn surrounding the mansion. She heard the steps echoing across the polished wood floor of the hallway and heading toward her room. She turned over slowly as Number Two entered. She fixed him with a solemn gaze, trying to remember what God's Word said concerning loving one's enemies. She was quoting Romans 12:19-21 as she watched him walk toward her.

Never take your own revenge, beloved, but leave room for the wrath of God, for it is written, Vengeance is Mine, I will repay, says the Lord. But if your enemy is hungry, feed him, and if he is thirsty, give him a drink; for in so doing, you will heap burning coals on his head. Do not be overcome by evil, but overcome evil with good.

"Hi, Number Two. I hope you are quite recovered from our little exercise earlier," she said with a sweet smile.

"You have got to be the craziest…"

Anna chose not to hear the rest of the sentence he was mumbling. He reached out to her hand and saw how swollen it was.

"You're going to have to get that looked at soon."

"Thanks for your concern, Two. May I call you Two? Or do you prefer Number?"

"What is wrong with you? Are you always this crazy?

"I'm not crazy at all, just at peace with my life and whatever the outcome might be because I know where I'm going when it ends."

"OK. That's enough of that!" he grumbled as he began disconnecting the ankle shackles.

Anna stood up and stretched out her muscles. It felt good to put one foot in front of the other in a normal way as they headed down the stairs. Number Two kept hold of the other wrist cuff and made sure to keep her close.

"Where are we going?"

"First we're going to the kitchen."

As they pushed through the door, Trais looked up in surprise. "Um. Hi? Is there something I can get for you?" he asked with his eyes averted. He found he couldn't look either of the people in the eye as they stood in the middle of his workspace.

"You have a big iron pot around here, don't you?

"Well, yeees. What kind of pot?"

"Something that will keep this wild woman from running away too quickly."

Trais didn't like being put in the position of finding anything to add to Anna's misery, but he felt he had no choice in order to maintain his cover, and hopefully, be on hand to rescue her when the opportunity presented itself. He reached down into a cabinet next to the commercial size stainless steel gas stove and pulled out a large iron Dutch oven.

"Here's the jambalaya pot. Will that do?"

"Yeah. That will be just fine. Keep the lid." Number Two worked the empty handcuff through the hole on the handle of the pot. "Perfect!" he said with a smile.

"Let's go." He swung the heavy pot at his side while Anna followed along like an injured puppy.

Chapter Forty-Seven

Trident helped Pelican pull a light pink tee-shirt over her head. Then she picked up the Mae West vest.

"I'm not wearing that thing! Wha... now... when... um... you know!"

"Yes, I know that you hate yellow and will never wear it, Pelican, but that's the only color these vests come in."

"Well, I just won't wear it then. It's ugly. You wear it." Pelican began kicking at her friend in frustration. "Everyone tells me what to do!"

"Pelican, we have an operation. I'm in charge now. We'll put a nice purple tunic over it and no one will even see it, but you need this flotation device for the operation."

"I've never needed that. You know my skill."

"Yes. Everyone who knows you knows that you have an extraordinary skill when it comes to floating on the ocean. Remember that story that Anna likes to tell?"

Pelican began smiling as the memory calmed her down. She always enjoyed this story.

Trident went on because she knew that her friend responded with more compliance when reminded of better times. "You were out on a holiday with your family. Your husband was building sandcastles with the children when

Anna looked up and saw you drifting farther and farther away. Your husband had to swim out and bring you back. You had actually fallen asleep on the surface of the ocean. They all said that you would have floated halfway from California to China before you woke from your nap."

They both enjoyed a chuckle as Doctor Karns looked on. He had a troubled expression on his face. "I wish I had been the one to rescue you. I wanted to be the one to make you happy."

"You were always... then, you know... had to. Necessary... for... um... Oh! Never mind. What were we talking about?"

"We were talking about how I always loved you and wished that I had been your husband. If all this works out as planned, would you consider finally marrying me?"

"Marry you! I don't even know who you are! Get away from me."

Doctor Karns sadly dropped his head. Edith patted him on the shoulder as he turned to shuffle out of the room, holding onto the handles of his wheelchair, using it as a walker. "You know she doesn't mean that. Five minutes from now, she'll love you again."

Just then, Pierce hurried into the room. "Sorry I'm running late. There was a lot to do. Are y'all almost ready? I don't have time to cook supper for the men so I'll just order them all pizza. We'll have to grab a snack on the way. Aunt Pelle, you look very nice in that purple tunic. Purple was always your color."

"You don't see what I have on underneath," she answered with a scowl.

"Ha! I never want to see your underwear, Aunt Pelle."

"It's not underwear. It's mission wear."

"Good deal!" Pierce grabbed the other vest and prodded his group of wobbly agents to the car. He was not at all confident about how all this might work out, but what choice did they have? Any one of them would have given their lives for Anna. He only hoped it wouldn't come to that.

Chapter Forty-Eight

Trais watched out the kitchen window helplessly as Anna was loaded into the car with the jambalaya pot attached to her handcuff. *How can anyone put someone into a little bateau with an iron pot attached to them?* This wasn't the mob. This was The Cooking School. Their job was to help the weak and oppressed by removing bad actors who were intent on destroying whole communities. They had been instrumental in stopping terrorists around the world. What were they coming to? Trais felt so disillusioned. He was ready to quit the whole business.

As soon as the dust settled behind the car, he left the mansion and jogged toward the pier. Which one should he choose? There were several along the bayou in Cocodrie. He had arranged for the boat the Canadians were using to be tied up further down toward the outlet to the gulf. The shrimp boat was closer.

He hoped everyone had gotten the messages and that they were boarding his dad's boat. He was as familiar with that boat as anyone and would find some way to intervene and save the hostages. That's why he had joined the organization. No matter how badly some chose to corrupt their noble cause, Trais was determined to make things better. He could still be the hero.

***

𝒟etective MacGregor was reeling in a catch. He knew it was a big one, but he hadn't been able to get a glimpse of it yet to determine what he had on his line. Detective Brown had already caught two nice redfish, but this was MacGregor's first bite. He hadn't wanted to give the fishing his full concentration because he was trying to keep the shrimp boat in his periphery the whole time.

"Come on! Reel him in!" Brown was jumping around the deep-sea fishing boat and shouting in his excitement. "I don't know when I've had this much fun! We're going to have to plan to do it again soon."

"We're not done with this one yet and you're already planning another," MacGregor huffed out as he struggled with the line. Finally, the fish popped out of the water and the angler quickly flipped him onto the deck of the boat. Both men scurried back out of the way as they saw the three-foot long bull shark thrashing around.

"Wow! Wow! Wow! Oh man! Did you ever catch a big one! Now how are we going to get rid of it?"

"I'm not touching it." The boat rocked gently from side to side with the dying shark's battering about. Neither man enjoyed watching such a beautiful, viable animal perish, but they couldn't figure out how to help it without getting injured.

Suddenly MacGregor got an idea. "Dump out the ice chest."

Brown ran to the ice chest and unceremoniously dumped ice and beer onto the deck. Cans rolled in every direction as the men slipped around in the melting ice. Each grabbed one end of the large Yeti and cautiously approached the flailing animal.

"Wait," ordered MacGregor. "We're going to get ourselves killed if we don't hold on a minute."

Brown looked at him questioningly and then noticed the shark's movements begin to slow. He understood the reasoning then. He hoped that they would be able to get the big fish back into the ocean at the right point between unconsciousness and death.

"Go!" Simultaneously, they dropped the ice chest sideways beside their prey and scooped it up. With one motion, they dumped the uninjured shark back into the ocean. Then they both slid down in the ice and sat there breathing deeply while the cold water soaked into their pants. Then they both began cracking up in relief.

"You know the worst part about all this?" Brown asked.

"What's that?"

"This is the best story of my life and I won't even be able to tell my wife." They both broke down in helpless laughter again.

As MacGregor was straightening up and wiping his streaming eyes, he looked toward the pier. The place where the shrimp boat had been previously tied up was now empty. He began to look frantically in every direction.

"What's up, dude?" asked Brown. "Are you trying to find your shark?" Brown began chuckling again but MacGregor no longer found any of it funny.

Chapter Forty-Nine

The bateau looked terribly small for the three of them, and the nature of a bateau, a flat-bottomed boat with practically no keel, made them notoriously difficult to handle. Anna looked down at the iron pot sitting in the bottom of the boat between her feet and understood how precarious her safety was.

They placed her in the front of the boat, it could hardly be called a bow, on the seat facing the rear. Number Two was on the back seat where the tiny outboard was connected by a couple of rusty bolts. Liam didn't even have a seat and was forced to sit in the bottom of the boat crowded in with her jambalaya pot. Liam and Anna were both a bit uncomfortable facing each other so closely. Had there been a nice jambalaya in that pot, it would have completely relieved any awkwardness.

Number Two dumped the fishing gear that had been in the boat into the water by the pier before he stepped aboard and settled onto the rear seat of the bateau. He flipped the propellor of the inconsequential-looking trawling motor into the water. It was so small, Anna was sure they wouldn't be able to make much time. The whole setup was made for a hobby fisherman to trawl around in the water. Looking at it, she concluded that they didn't intend to go far. It took several pulls on the rope before the motor sputtered into action.

She didn't know the exact time, but could tell that the sun would set in about an hour or so. It was beginning to look a little dusky on the water. Visibility was at its worst under these conditions. She gazed hopefully around for another boat, preferably the Coast Guard.

Their little craft puttered out into the middle of the canal. She closed her eyes and spoke a silent prayer. *Lord, if it is in Your will that I can be delivered from this without anyone being hurt, I pray that you will do it. But You do all things well, O Lord, and my life and the lives of all I love are safely hidden under the shadow of Your wing.* As the Lord's peace entered her heart, a sweet smile adorned her face. She opened her eyes to see Liam looking at her with wonder.

***

As the dusk was deepening, Anna was starting to become concerned; too much time was passing. What was the delay? Did something happen to them? Was that the mutter of another boat engine? Its deep, thrumming noise was approaching from behind where she sat, but it was hard to be sure. Soundwaves traveled over water in an unpredictable way.

Then she heard Number Two mumble, "Looks like them. The message in the recipe indicated spicy shrimp kabob and that certainly looks like a shrimp boat. Not that I know much about them. I'm sure Trais knows. I suppose I should have asked him to describe one to me, but I didn't want to hazard giving too much away. It's got weird spikes sticking out of it. I guess they're to hold shrimp nets or something. Looks kinda cool."

Anna was surprised to hear Number Two's tone. It was almost like he was enjoying himself. She turned her head around to get a look. "Yes. That's a shrimp boat. Those 'spikes' as you called them, are for the nets, as you correctly surmised. They're called trawling beams."

"I didn't ask for a lesson in maritime lore, missy," Number Two growled.

Well, there went that good mood. This man switched back and forth so much that it was difficult to gauge how best to deal with him. His unpredictability was one of the things that made him come across as so dangerous. She looked at Liam who gently put his index finger to his lips. Was he trying to help her? Her heart fluttered with hope.

Chapter Fifty

Pierce finished writing his apology note about supper and promised that pizza for everyone would be delivered at six, already paid for, tip included. *That should do it. Who doesn't love pizza?*

He caught up with everyone in the process of loading into his car. Doctor Karns was using a new wheeled walker Pierce was able to get out of a surplus closet there at the shelter. It made it so much easier to have fewer wheelchairs to deal with. He wasn't as steady on his feet as Pierce would have liked, but as long as they stayed on even ground and took their time, they were able to manage.

He scooped up Pelican and deposited her on the back seat next to the doctor as his mom settled into the front passenger seat. Once the wheelchair and walker were both folded up and stowed in the trunk, which was like putting together a complicated Tetris puzzle, they were able to get under way.

Pierce was getting exasperated. It seemed like everything was going in slow motion. Dealing with his own mature mother sometimes tried his patience, but dealing with three aging people in various stages of physical and mental decline, he found to be a greater trial than many of the hazardous missions he had undertaken.

Once again, he tried to keep his foot from getting too heavy on the gas pedal. He couldn't spare the time to be stopped by the police, so it was better to avoid that at any cost, even of sticking to pushing the speed limit to only five-miles-per-hour over instead of the ten or fifteen he would have preferred.

He finally pulled up in front of the shrimp boat at exactly six. He was supposed to be meeting the Canadians at six. This was frustrating, and then he realized that the way was too uneven for Doctor Karns to make it using the walker. He had to load Pelican into her chair, get her aboard the boat and seated on a bench. He asked Mr Fuqua to go to the car and transport the doctor onto the boat in the now available wheelchair. His mom helped by pushing the walker aboard, and then they were finally ready.

The shrimp boat was chugging down the waterway as fast as Mr Fuqua could push her. He explained that he could get her up to about forty knots out in the open gulf, but that wasn't allowed down the canal. At twenty-five knots, Pierce felt like they were crawling along the surface of the water as the sun dipped closer to the horizon and a hazy mist of rain began to cloud his vision.

They chugged past a nice little Bluewater sports fishing boat. Pierce was able to recognize the two men on board as his detective friends. They turned and followed at a distance of about a football field.

***

"Where are we going?" asked Brown. "Aren't we going to head back before this rain gets any worse?"

MacGregor breathed a deep sigh of relief at regaining view of the shrimp boat. "Something looks a tad suspicious. Let's just follow a couple of minutes and see what turns up. You want to make the excuse you told your wife more plausible, don't you? If we can, you can keep your fish and your great fish story."

"That will make it worth something. Hope we catch some bad guys!"

***

"It looks like your family doesn't think much of you, little missy," Number Two snickered. He was hiding his aggravation at having to sit out in the middle of the canal, not knowing when his intended prey might show up. They discussed the way the boat looked as it drew closer, with the smoke from its diesel engine puffing into the air as the clouds grew more threatening and the light drizzle was beginning to make them uncomfortable.

Anna felt the kaleidoscope of butterflies starting to have a party in her stomach. Was this fear or excitement? Were the butterflies a result of the danger or the result of knowing that Pierce was getting closer. How would he look? What would he do?

Again, she felt a smile form on her lips that she couldn't quite control. Neither of the men on the bateau noticed her anyway. They had all their focus over her left shoulder where the ocean-going vessel captained by a man with many years of experience was bearing down on them. They suddenly felt intimidated. Number Two puffed out his chest and pulled out a gun.

Chapter Fifty-One

Pierce's voice reverberated along the canal and bounced off the trees on either side causing some distortion, but Anna still found it a thrilling sound. But her heart froze at his words. "We have the one you want onboard with us here."

"OK, well, I hope she can swim. Push her off into the water and my man will swim over to her and help her get back to my boat. Then we'll push this little lady into the water and you can help her back onto your boat."

"Look, we have a hook on the end of this trawling beam. We can hook the woman onto that and set her into your boat. Then you can put the hook onto Anna and we'll bring her up onto our boat. Doesn't that sound like a better idea?"

"Long as we get our hostage first. Go ahead."

Pierce turned to Pelican. "Make us all proud by living up to your name again Aunt Pelle. You know what to do as soon as you hit the water. Show everyone how great you can float. Just do what you do and everything will turn out fine. I have a little surprise for you in a minute."

"A surprise? Is it cake?"

"It's better than cake. It's the ride of your life!"

"OK!" Pelican said as the hook through the loop on the back of her life vest lifted her into the air. The trawling beam was directed up by the small electric motor attached to it. Then the beam was sent out to the side of the boat with Pelican dangling over the water.

"Wheeeee!" she yelled as, with the push of a button, the hook opened up, and she dropped the ten-feet into the water. The extra buoyancy provided by the instant inflation of her Mae West vest caused her to pop right up onto the surface where she promptly rolled over onto her back and began to enjoy one of her favorite activities. This had been denied to her for too many years. Pelican was floating like a beachball.

As Anna looked on, her smile widened. She knew how much her mama loved the water and how capable she was once she was deluged. It occurred to her how she had forgotten this fact. In her unrealistic desire to protect her mother, she had eliminated the one environment where her physical restrictions were no longer limitations for her. She wasn't like most people. Even with the loss of so many faculties, she retained this natural talent. She could float across the ocean while taking a nap.

Number Two hesitated in surprise for a second, then he raised his gun toward Anna. "Your mama is going to drown soon, and I have taken no pleasure in your company. If my deepest desire to watch your mother die at my hand is denied me, I will at least derive that pleasure from you."

Before the gun discharged, Liam dived in front of Anna. He took the bullet intended for her, and with the momentum, toppled across her lap into the water.

"You lunatic!" Number Two screamed at Liam. "What did you hope to accomplish?"

Number Two looked at Liam struggling in the water for a second and then aimed the gun back at Anna. "All he bought for you with his life was a couple of seconds."

At that moment, a shot was fired from the deck of the shrimp boat. Anna saw it enter the side of his chest. With a stunned expression, his body began tilting, tilting dangerously. It seemed he was in slow motion, and then, with greater momentum, he went over the edge of the bateau into the Intercoastal Canal. She felt like she was made of stone as she watched one man struggling in the water on her right side and one on her left.

Liam was barely holding his head above the brackish water as he said, "Lord Jesus, please forgive my sins and receive me into your kingdom." Sinking down toward the muddy bottom of the canal, a hymn that his granny sang to him as a young boy played through his mind:

When peace like a river attendeth my way,
When sorrows like sea billows roll,
Whatever my lot, Thou hast taught me to say,
It is well, it is well with my soul.

The joy he felt in that last fleeting moment was greater than any he thought possible in all his lifetime.

Anna then looked to her left and saw Number Two struggling to stay afloat, with cursing and garbled threats, as he began descending down into his liquid grave. She thought of the two thieves who died beside Christ, one crucified on His right and one on His left, who saw all that He said and did. While one was convicted and saved, the other died in his sin. She marveled again at God's amazing grace.

Chapter Fifty-Two

John was driving the speedboat just as quickly as he dared with Manny next to him peering through binoculars. Visibility was poor and getting worse with the drizzling rain getting heavier and the clouds getting darker.

"I'm surprised the Coast Guard doesn't come after us with the conditions getting as they are," John said.

"Up ahead! I see the shrimp boat but that's all I can see."

They had buzzed past the two police detectives in their fishing boat without even slowing down. The detectives grabbed onto the gunwale as the heavy wake from the speedboat crashed into the side of their boat.

"Let's go!" Brown yelled.

"Hold on just a minute," MacGregor answered. "They look like they're stopping."

He was watching the speedboat and the two dark-skinned men through his binoculars. Manny was pulling out what looked like a large boogie board and attaching it to the back of the boat with a yellow cord. John jumped out and climbed onto it, holding tightly to the two handles molded into the sides of the bright yellow board. Manny eased on the gas, and the boat picked up speed with John billowing water off the back of the boogie board.

"OK," Brown said. "Can we go after them now?"

"Let's just go slowly and hang back to see what's up."

The speedboat rounded a shrimp boat with its trawling beam sticking out the side. MacGregor could see what looked like the man on the boogie board scooping up a large object from the water and placing it between his knees.

"Looks like some kind of drug deal if you ask me," Brown asserted.

"Not sure what's happening, but it does look suspicious. Let's catch up to that speedboat. We'll come back to the shrimp boat later." MacGregor recognized Fuqua's shrimp boat and knew where to find it, but he didn't recognize the other boat or the men on it. Maybe this whole thing had just been some kind of drug dealer's charade and they had been playing him all along.

They skirted the shrimp boat and headed down toward the opening of the gulf. When they emerged around a bend, they saw that the speedboat had stopped and the boogie board was being pulled in. They drew their service weapons as they approached.

"Police! Show us your hands!"

At that, Pelican looked around and saw the detectives. "Put those things away before you hurt someone!"

"Yes, ma'am," they both said as they holstered their handguns. They recognized the elderly lady but not the two ruffians who had her. They didn't want to cause the men to hurt their hostage so they found it prudent to play along.

"Ma'am, are you all right?"

"Never better! I'm having the time of my life, but let me tell you, I don't approve of the color of this thing they put me on. What's it called? Anyway, everyone knows I don't like yellow. Next time make sure it's purple. Now, let's go get my fiancé and go on our honeymoon."

Manny looked at the two strong officers and asked if they would help lift their passenger onto their boat.

"How do I know you're telling the truth?"

Manny pulled out his cellphone and dialed Edith's number. "I have a couple of detectives here who think we're kidnapping your friend. Would you like to talk with them?"

After Detective MacGregor handed the phone back to Manny, he and Detective Brown helped the two Haitians load the wet, slippery, senior agent onto the speedboat.

"It looks like everything's under control here. We'll let you all go about your business."

Brown looked at MacGregor with confusion. "We're going to just let them go without checking further into this?"

"I've already checked the rest of these people out. It's a long story, one you can't share with your wife. We'll work out what you can tell her. We don't want to be banned from going fishing again. Now, let's get this boat back. Hand me a beer, will you?"

Chapter Fifty-Three

Anna sat immobilized in the bow of the bateau with her back to the larger boat, still in wonder about what she had just seen. She was in awe of how God had placed her in the position of being a witness to Liam before it was too late for him. Her heart was rejoicing in knowing that she would see him again in eternity, and they would both give glory to their Savior for what He had done for them. Tears were streaming down her face as she was wrapped up in a world of glory giving praise to her God and King.

She was startled out of her reverie by a bump on the boat and the voice she had been waiting to hear again. "Anna, jump out to me and we'll swim to the shrimp boat. You're safe now."

Anna lifted her still-shackled hand and indicated the weighty pot attached to the other end. Pierce examined the situation and then his eyes moved over her and noticed her injuries. Her eye was swollen along with her cheek and into her chin. Her wrist appeared to be broken. He felt the heat rise to his face as his anger bubbled over.

"Those sons of…" He checked his speech. "They got what they deserved!"

Anna just looked at him in pity realizing that he would not be able to understand her sorrow for the loss of their lives. "Can you get me onto the ship?"

Pierce didn't correct her use of the word, ship, knowing that wasn't technically what it was. "I'm wearing an inflatable life vest. It should be able to hold us both." He reached in and picked up the iron pot. He then gently pulled Anna's uninjured arm around his neck and clutched the pot to his chest so as not to put weight on the cuffs and cause her further pain. She gingerly slipped off the bateau and onto the strength provided by Pierce.

He paddled with his free arm while he and Anna synchronized their kicking feet to propel them toward the boat. "I think this must be our first dance, Pierce." They both giggled in nervous delight at finally being together. As they approached the ladder up the side of the shrimp boat, Pierce could see that it wouldn't be easy to hoist her up.

"Hey!" he yelled. "Send down the trawling beam."

Mr Fuqua instantly saw the dilemma and complied. Pierce struggled to remove his belt with one hand and then the two of them worked to get it fastened under Anna's arms. Pierce then fastened the hook to the back of it. "You're going to have to hold onto this pot with your good arm. This isn't going to be easy; do you think you can manage it?"

Anna nodded her head yes just as the beam began lifting her into the air. As the long pole shifted directions to bring it back in toward the boat, the pot slipped out of

Anna's grasp. The weight of the falling pot yanked so hard on her shoulder that she let out a scream. Pierce started scrambling as quickly as he could in the bulky, inflated vest and hoisted himself onto the deck just as Anna was deposited next to him.

Doctor Karns called out to Edith to help him get to Anna's side. She eased him to a sitting position next to Anna, who was crying and gasping in pain.

"Her shoulder is dislocated. I need help to get it back in."

Mr Fuqua and Pierce looked at each other.

"We'll do whatever you say. I just hope we don't make things worse." Pierce was fighting back his own tears at seeing Anna in such distress.

They didn't notice the sound of the speedboat approaching. Manny stuck his head over the top of the railing and called out, "What's going on?"

Doctor Karns was relieved to see more help arrive because he didn't think he could count on Pierce to be able to do what was necessary under the circumstances. "Mr Fuqua, you'll need to grab her around the chest and hold tight. Manny, come over here. Anna's dislocated her shoulder and you have to lend a hand to get it set right."

"Oh! No problem. I've done this several times."

The doctor let out a sigh of relief at having someone who was experienced in what was, essentially, battlefield medicine. With one last yelp of pain, Anna felt instant relief as her shoulder was pulled back into the socket.

"I can take care of this other problem too." Manny eyed her handcuffs and the pot.

Manny was busy unlocking the handcuffs and the doctor was wrapping Anna's broken wrist in a temporary splint, as Pelican was brought back on board. John tied the speedboat up to the side of the shrimp boat and joined the little celebratory group.

"I know just what to do with this pot," Pierce declared as he carried it to the galley. "Anyone want some jambalaya for supper?"

Chapter Fifty-Four

Trais had sprinted to the pier as soon as the car was out of sight. When he found the shrimp boat gone, he hurried down the canal to the location where the bateau had been tied. It was also gone. At the edge of the water, he peered down the bayou.

Visibility was getting more difficult as the clouds got darker and a mist of rain blew into his eyes. He thought he could just make out the shrimp boat further along toward the gulf.

He tried to catch up to the boats from the shore, frequently having to move further inland to avoid obstacles such as swamps, alligators and heavy foliage. When he emerged, he had passed them by, and was nearing the outlet into the gulf in a secluded place where there were no piers.

He had no idea what he was doing or how he could help. All he could do was watch helplessly from the shore. With the poor visibility, he couldn't quite figure out what was happening, but eventually, a speedboat zoomed past. Then a deep-sea fishing boat broke the wake in its pursuit of the speedboat.

They were soon both out of sight. When he heard gunshots, he feared the worse. He fell to his knees and cried out, "Oh God! Please help! Please help! Please help!" That was all he could think, but in this desperation, the only thing he could do was plead with the God he had recently ridiculed.

His emotions were all jumbled up. He was disappointed that he couldn't use this situation to prove himself to The Cooking School, to Pierce, and mostly, to his father. He was fearful for the lives of those he cared most about. He was worried that the Canadians would come back and kill him too. He was sorry for making fun of Anna's faith. And he was very sorry for his own sins. He just couldn't help the flood of words that poured out of his mouth in a prayer. "God, I'm sorry. Please forgive me. Please help these people. I don't care if I never get to be a hero. I don't care if I never get to be anyone special or if anyone ever looks up to me. I just want to be able to trust in You."

Trais continued to stand on shore and try to watch as he prayed. The sound of agonized screams bounced across the water and bombarded his eardrums, causing his heart to pound like a kettle drum. He heard before he saw the speedboat return and then, after another sharp scream, everything began to settle down.

He noticed the bateau washing in the current toward where he was standing just as his nostrils picked up the familiar smell of jambalaya on the stove. He dove into the canal and swam toward the bateau. In no time, he paddled it out to his father's boat.

When he climbed aboard the shrimp boat, he didn't see anyone on deck but his dad. "Where is everyone?"

"Oh!" Mr Fuqua yelled in delight as he bounded toward his son to wrap him in a big bear hug. "They're downstairs drying off, which is what you're going to do now too. Then we'll all eat and catch up on how every one of us played an important part in getting these fine people safe."

Trais' kettledrum heart settled into a nice, peaceful snare drum as he grinned under the warmth of his father's acknowledgement.

After everyone changed into dry clothes, they ate their fill of the best jambalaya any of them could remember. Then they fixed sleeping arrangements on board for the night. Tomorrow would send them all off in different directions again. They weren't quite finished making sure of the safety of the aging Pelican.

Anna and Pierce were in sleeping bags on the topside along with Mr Fuqua and Trais. The bunks were given to the people whose old bones couldn't well tolerate the hard deck of the boat. Anna giggled and said, "We haven't slept together since we were toddlers, cousin Pierce." It was such a relief to be able to laugh about something together again.

Just as they were drifting off, they heard, "Who do you think you are? Get your hands off me, you dirty old man!"

Chapter Fifty-Five

"When are we ever going to get there?"

"Remember, I told you it takes six hours to get to Mobile. We're only about halfway there." Doctor Karns was patient with Pelican. Manny didn't know how he did it. She was starting to get on his nerves. It was like being with a spoiled five-year-old.

After only a few more minutes, "Aren't we almost there yet?"

"No, dear. You just asked that."

"I'm so tired of this!"

"I know. This is very tiring, but honey, you love the ocean and you love boat rides. Smell the nice sea air. You're so excited to go to Mobile and take a cruise. We talked about all this."

"You're making that up, and why is this ride so long? Stop! Just stop! I'm getting out now."

"Have you learned to walk on water, dear?"

"Humppf! You've forgotten how well I can float. I'm just going to float home. They're waiting for me to get supper, you know. The kids want me to cook. They're used to my bad cooking."

"All right, my darling. You can cook soon. These nice men are taking us home now. You just relax. Why don't you take a little nap? That will make the time pass faster."

Pelican leaned back and shut her eyes. In less than fifteen minutes, her eyes popped back open. She looked around at the unchanging ocean. "Are we there yet?"

It seemed like they went right back through the same conversation all over again. Manny and John didn't know where the doctor got his patience. They had both been through some horrific experiences following the earthquake in their own island nation. The UN and the corrupt politicians squandered the money that was to have been used for rebuilding while the citizens were reduced to scavenging anything they could just to keep the rain off their heads. Cholera was running rampant with no end in sight for the distress, and yet, here they were transporting these spoiled rich people.

But they had made a promise to Aunt Edith. She had certainly done a lot for their family. She had arrived a decade earlier and helped build a new school with her own money and her own labor of love. They would do this for her. They tamped down their annoyance and carried on.

Manny revved the boat to even greater speeds, trying to end this trifling ordeal. He and John were to take the cruise with the couple so that they could see them safely to their destination. At least they'd be in a different stateroom.

***

After the shrimp boat tied off at their usual pier, everyone said their goodbyes and headed to Pierce's Camry. Mr Fuqua picked up his cellphone to tell his other two sons that the vacation was over and they were going to head back out into the gulf. They still had work to do no matter what kind of intrigue was going on in the rest of the world. He actually felt a little sadness that the adventure was over. He shook his head at his own foolishness, but couldn't help a little smile of satisfaction.

After dropping Edith and Anna off at the hospital to get her wrist set, Pierce pulled into the rear parking lot of his too long abandoned restaurant. The first order of business was to print up new signs stating a *Grand Reopening* after redecorating. He and Trais would have a lot to do in order to make the turnaround as short as possible. He couldn't help worrying about Anna, even though he was now firmly convinced of how well she could take care of herself. The thought flashed through his mind, *She'll just pray about it.*

Pierce called Todd at the homeless shelter to apologize to him again about not being there to cook. He was relieved to hear that a newly discharged inmate had some great skills in that department. Todd was delighted about the offer for a free fine dining experience once the restaurant was up and running again. It didn't seem like anything upset the man much. Pierce was glad to know someone who was so solid and unflappable.

***

Detective MacGregor was, thankfully, at his desk, when Edith put the call through. "Detective, could you please do me a little favor?"

"Sure, anything!"

"Well, I'm here at the emergency room with Anna, and the doctor keeps asking a bunch of questions. He rightly thinks something suspicious has happened and we don't want him digging into it, do we? I don't want to use your name and tell him that we filed a report about the 'mugging' in which she was hurt without asking you."

"No. That's fine. Just give him this number. I'll vouch for y'all. You've both been through enough. Is everything going OK?"

"Yes. We're fine. We found a new nursing home for Pelle and Phil. Everything is working out getting them settled. All the bad guys are out of the picture."

"I sure wish you could tell me more about this organization you worked for."

"Detective MacGregor, trust me. There are some things you just really don't want to know."

"I think you're underestimating my sense of curiosity."

"Ha. Maybe I am, Detective. We'll talk again."

"Looking forward to it, ma'am," he said, hanging up.

Chapter Fifty-Six

"Two flights to Belize, please."

"Will that be roundtrip or one-way?"

"Better make it one-way for now. We don't know how long our business might take."

"Here you go. Enjoy your flight."

Edith was taking great pleasure in pampering Anna after how much she had been through. Edith had loved her little namesake from the first time she saw her tiny, pink, infant face, but now their bond was closer than ever.

Anna was wearing a pair of large sunglasses to camouflage the deepening bruises on her face, her shoulder that was recovering from dislocation was in a sling and her other wrist was in a cast up to her elbow. Edith had insisted on pushing her through the New Orleans airport in a wheelchair.

"There's nothing wrong with my legs, Aunt Edith."

"No, my girl, but your body has been through quite a trauma and you shouldn't exert yourself in any way. This vacation is just what you need."

"But Belize? Why Belize?"

"Just relax and try to enjoy our little surprise, won't you?" Edith was so happy to be able to spring this on her niece.

"First class! Aunt Edith. So extravagant!"

"But I love you extravagantly, my dear." It felt so good to share this mutual love that the bond in Jesus Christ had given the two women. Edith didn't think she had ever been happier, and judging by the sweet smile on her face, Anna was quite happy herself.

After a six-hour flight, they were touching down in a tropical paradise. "Why exactly did you choose Belize, Aunt Edith?"

"The Haitians recommended it."

"Oh! That was nice of them. I guess they know something about the local attractions?"

"One attraction especially."

"Where are we staying?"

"We are actually going to one of the little islands offshore." An airport concierge helped them load their luggage into a cab, which had them to the coast in no time. As they arrived at the dock, they could see a large cruise ship anchored out a short distance from the beach. "The harbor is too shallow for a ship of this size. We have a boat reserved to pick up the rest of our party, and then take us all to the destination."

***

The boat that would take the party of four out to the island pulled up alongside several others that were queued up at the floating dock next to the cruise ship. After sitting and waiting for a few minutes, passengers began to disembark from the cruise ship. Among them were two silver-haired tourists who were being pushed in wheelchairs by two imposing men in dreadlocks. The other passengers were joyfully throwing confetti into the air.

As they neared, Anna called out, "Confetti! That's quite an elaborate celebration just for a cruise!

"We're celebrating a wedding!" Doctor Karns called out happily.

"Oh, Mama! Seriously? Seriously! What were you th—" She felt a sharp elbow in her side.

"Don't you dare spoil this for them. They've waited nearly fifty-years to finally be together. This is the fourth happiest day of your mother's life."

"Fourth?"

"How many children does she have?"

Understanding dawned on Anna and she smiled. "Oh, yes! The fourth happiest day of her life." Anna rushed toward her mother and gave her a big hug and kiss.

"I don't know what all the fuss is about," Mama said with a huff.

Doctor Karns was beaming. He wouldn't let anything cast a shadow over his elation — even a grumpy bride.

Chapter Fifty-Seven

They arrived at the small, unnamed island near Water Cay, another tiny, barely habitable island off the coast of Belize. There was a lovely, triangle shaped beach sticking out of the south side of the atoll into the ocean. It appeared that most of the rest of the island was jungle, unbroken almost to the water's edge. Anna felt nothing but trepidation as she tried to peer through the gloom of the dense forest.

There was no discernable place for the small vessel to land, yet they proceeded right up to the shore. At the last moment, she saw an inlet, well hidden by the surrounding terrain.

They tied off at a precarious bamboo and plank pier. Anna would have been afraid to set foot on it, had not Manny and John shown such confidence in its structural integrity.

"Here we are!" Manny shouted with joy.

They watched as an antique looking vehicle came into view. It reminded Anna of World War Two ambulance trucks she had seen on TV. Two young men and one beautiful young woman alighted from the vehicle.

All of them were as dark as Manny and John and all were dressed in various shades of pastel hospital scrubs.

They gave each other extravagant hugs and spoke excitedly in Creole French.

John put his arm around the young lady. "I would like to introduce my sister Phara and my favorite, most intelligent countrymen. This is Daniel and the tall lanky one here we call Junior. It is their job to make everything perfect for you." At that, the men unloaded canvas stretchers.

"Is that really necessary?" Anna asked.

"We have no handicap accessible vehicles so we must transport our patients this way."

They walked down the pier and spoke briefly with Doctor Karns. He nodded his head and then climbed onto the stretcher with Manny's help and lay back for the ride up to the vehicle.

Then they returned for their lady patient. She absolutely refused to cooperate with the conveyance they had brought to her. Finally, Anna approached and used the only method that had worked on her mother since she had Alzheimer's. She lied through her teeth.

"Mama. You see these wonderful people here on this island? They've been waiting for you to come and rule them. They've been without a leader for so many years. When they found out that you would consider coming to be their new queen, they sent out this welcoming committee. Here is your private palanquin." She indicated with a flourish. "They will carry you to your throne."

Pelican beamed brightly as they helped her to sit upright on the stretcher. She waved just like Queen

Elizabeth as they made their way to the truck. "I don't like my royal vehicle. You must paint it in gold leaf."

"Yes, my liege." Junior smiled.

Soon the truck made its slow, bumpy way up the track that couldn't be called a road by any definition. Anna watched Mama; even though she was being jostled about on the rough road, she sat in satisfaction, beaming in her royal splendor.

They neared the center of the island where the trees thinned out. There was a type of lagoon or pond in the middle of the island surrounded by thatched huts. There were date palms, coconut palms, flowers and fruit trees growing all around. As they got closer, Anna could see that it was an entire village complete with stores, beauty shop, restaurants and other types of entertainment, even a bar and a small theater.

Then she saw safety barricades, smooth sidewalks, and ramps. There were elderly people in wheelchairs, using walkers and canes, and some just strolling along arm in arm. Everywhere she looked, she saw attendants in their pastel scrubs attending to the residents. It dawned on her. This was a perfect retirement village with assisted living and who knew what else.

She looked with wonder at her Haitian friends. "How long have y'all known about this place?"

"Most of our lives. Our family runs it. Some of it is a cover for The Cooking School and some of it is a functioning retirement home. You will find several of our retirees living here."

Anna looked at Edith. "Did you know about this place?"

"I didn't at first, but had you come to me with your mama's problems, we would have made inquiries."

"The hit on Mama…"

"It does not apply here. She's safe. Nothing she says will create a leak in our organization."

Relief flooded Anna. For the first time since she had made the awful decision to place her mother in that nursing home, she felt at peace. She should have known not to do anything that didn't bring peace to her heart. That was one way the Holy Spirit guided His own. But looking back on the whole experience, how many had come to Christ or received a witness through this difficulty?

"Manny, is there a chapel here?"

"Of course! We have everything. Let us get these newlyweds settled into their new home."

Pelican looked at Doctor Karns. "This is our honeymoon?"

"Yes, my love."

"It's very nice. Can we stay forever?"

"Whatever you want, my sweet."

"Who do you think you're sweet-talking? Your sweet! I'll bet you don't even know my name. I'll bet you don't even know where I was born."

"You were born in Miami and your name is Rebecca."

Mama turned her honeyed smile on the doctor. "I don't know who you are, but you sure do know how to flatter a lady! Let's get checked in. It's time we had a little privacy."

Doctor Karns put his arm around the love of his life and looked back at Anna and Edith.

"Did he just wink?" Anna shuddered.

"I believe he did, my dear."

What is True

My real-life daddy truly did have to swim out into the ocean and wake Mama up to bring her to shore as she was dozing and floating away on the tide off the coast of California where he was stationed in the Navy.

The towns of Cocodrie and Dulac are real places located where they should be along the bayous of south Louisiana. The culture and the cuisine are all true as well. The church on Camp Street is a real church. It was recently bought by Beyonce to use to help inner city youth in New Orleans. My grandfather was the pastor there in the 1970s.